BLOOD OATH

MAFIA ELITE, BOOK 2

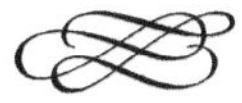

AMY MCKINLEY

ARROWSCOPE PRESS, LLC

(*p*) **ISBN-13**: 978-1-951919-12-2

(*e*) **ISBN-13**: 978-1-951919-11-5

Publisher: Arrowscope Press, LLC; www.arrowscopepress.com

Editing— Kate Birdsall, Line Editor, Taylor Anhalt, Proofreader, Red Adept Editing

Cover Design—T.E. Black Designs; www.teblackdesigns.com

Author photo provided by—Brookelyn Anhalt of lovely.life.photography; https://www.facebook.com/LovelyLifePhotography-102253596490708

Interior Formatting & Design— Arrowscope Press, LLC; www.arrowscopepress.com

THE FAMILY

Chicago Outfit
Italian American Mafia

Caruso Family

- Antonio – (father, boss)
- Maria (first wife, deceased, Max's Mom)
- Nicole (second wife (Tony's Mom, Elena's adopted Mom))
- Tony (son)
- Maximus "Max" (son)
- Elena (adopted daughter)
- Vito (advisor to boss)
- *Maria's family from Italy*
- Salvio "Sal" (cousin)
- Cristiano (cousin)
- Tommasso (cousin)
- Aunt Rosa (lives in Sicily)

Brambilla Family

- Benito (boss)
- Julia (wife, deceased)
- Liliana "Lil" (daughter)
- Leonardo (underboss, cousin)
- Dino (advisor to boss)
- Eva (cousin)
- Vincenzo (Julia's Sicilian father, Liliana's grandfather)

La Rosa Family

- Robert (boss)
- Angela (wife)
- Marco (son, underboss)
- Nico (son)
- Trey (son)
- Sofia (daughter)
- Maso (boss's brother, advisor)
- Tom (captain)

Vitale Family

- Emilio (boss)
- Alessia (wife)
- Enzo (son, underboss)
- Emiliana "Em" (daughter)
- Aldo (advisor to boss)

- Renato "Ren" (captain)

Rossi Family

- Frank (father, boss)
- Carla (mother, deceased)
- Alfonso (son, deceased)
- Stefano (son, underboss)
- Camila (daughter)
- Marissa (daughter, deceased)
- Drago (advisor to the boss)

Russian Mafia
Pavlov Bratva

Pavlov Bratva

- Yuri (boss)
- Mischa (wife)
- Ivan (eldest son, underboss)
- Victor "Vic" (son)
- Katya (angel of death, assassin)

CHAPTER ONE

SOFIA

We're raised to love as hard as we war. There are monsters in all of us.

Dresses in every hue and style were strewn over the table, waiting for me to choose. I could lose myself in fashion design and creation, my passion, and sometimes even block out the dark world I existed in. Born into one of the Five Families of the Italian American Mafia, I was no stranger to pain, blood, and death. The omnipresent sense of loss was the worst. It weighed on my soul. At night, haunting images of those close to me who had died would return to torment my dreams. One of my best friends, Marissa, had died in December of our senior year of college. And her brother Alfonso's death when we were children took our innocence with him.

But in my studio, I could block my reality, if only for a little while.

With pins pinched between my lips, I circled Eva, Lil's cousin and one of my closest friends, along with Emiliana. Dropping to my knees, I bent to the hem of the sexy-as-hell red evening gown, transferring the pins to the fabric, marking where I needed to shorten it by half an inch. I rocked back onto my heels then smiled up at Eva. "You're going to own the runway in this dress." She was a knockout with a body that stopped men in their tracks—literally. I'd witnessed it a time or two.

Eva pursed her full red lips then pivoted from side to side in the mirror in front of her as I got to my feet. A rare flash of self-consciousness clouded her dark eyes. "Are you sure? I'm not runway worthy."

"Christ, Eva." I rolled my eyes. "Remember your bloodline. We can do whatever the hell we want. And I don't want starving models wearing my line. With your curves, this dress is you."

A half smile curved her lips, and she tilted her head, her dark mass of long brown hair spilling over her right shoulder from the movement. "True. I forget sometimes. We're not royalty, not like you."

She was referring to herself and the other cousins. "Stop. All it means is that the target on your back isn't quite as large. Embrace it." Eva was the life of the party, but for some reason, she'd shown insecurity about being a cousin and not a Mafia princess like Liliana, Emiliana, and me. There had once been three more of us, but Marissa had been murdered, another was assumed to be dead after being married off to a Russian—I repressed a shudder—and then there was Elena. Everyone thought she was dead too.

She wasn't. I was one of the only people who knew the truth.

"I'm counting on you, Eva." I paused in adjusting the bodice. "I want you in Milan with me, wearing this dress."

"When would I ever turn down a trip to Milan?" She grinned, and I had to laugh with her.

Eva was a party girl, and Fashion Week would be another opportunity to have fun. She did a little shimmy that drew attention to her perfectly round ass and the way her breasts were close to spilling out of the crisscross bodice, exactly how I'd designed the dress. "I can already see the paparazzi."

I rolled my eyes, knowing she would eat the publicity up. "You'll flirt with anything with a pulse, even death."

"Mmm, I'd make an exceptional honeypot."

Bile climbed my throat, and I ducked my head so she wouldn't see my reaction to the term of a Russian spy who gained intel by using their body. "We're not Russian."

"Oh!" Her fingers curled around my arm in an excited grip. "Remember Ivan Pavlov? The super-hot Russian who went to our college that one semester?"

Suspicious for sure. None of us had forgotten him. "What about him?" I couldn't have kept the wariness from my voice if I wanted to. I motioned for her to turn so I could unzip her.

"I saw him the other day." Eva stepped out of the dress, and I hung it on the clothing rack with a few others that needed alterations. "Hey, is Enzo coming to Milan?"

I shivered at all the blows she was inadvertently delivering. Ivan wasn't sexy—he was dangerous, and I didn't like him being in town. Nothing good would come of that. The double punch of her mentioning a member of the Russian Mafia and Enzo in the same conversation did unpleasant things to my mind. I traced the scar on my right palm with my index finger, traveling back in my memory as I touched its slightly raised edge.

My studio faded, and in its place, soft grass tickled my little-girl sandal-clad toes. The sun made everything brighter, more exciting, as I slipped from my mom's arms and ran to play with Enzo by the swings. Tony and Alfonso were with him. Tony was mean. I tried to stay away from him because he pushed me down a lot.

My brothers didn't want to come, which made me happy. If they had, Enzo might not play with me. I worried he still wouldn't because of the other boys. Alfonso didn't like girls, even though he had two sisters, Marissa and Camila, who were on the swings, and I waved. Elena skipped over, her ponytail swinging from side to side.

"I like your dress!" Marissa shouted, pumping her legs to go higher.

My smile widened. It was a pretty dress, one of my favorites with its ballerina skirt and tiny flowers. Liliana would have loved it, too, if she'd been able to come play.

I caught Alfonso's smirk and Enzo grabbing his arm when he made a move toward me. Alfonso's papa didn't stop him from pushing his sisters or me. That was why I liked Enzo so much. He was nice to me, like my brothers. One day, I would marry him.

"Where's Em?" I stopped in front of Enzo, careful to stay out of Alfonso's reach and far from Tony.

"Home sick." He shrugged then pushed Alfonso in the direction of the slides. Tony followed.

I tried not to be sad. Then Camila fell and burst into tears. Her mom came over, pulled her into her arms, then called Alfonso and Marissa. I rocked onto my toes, unsure of what to do. Elena edged away from them, her eyes teary. Camila was bleeding. She'd scraped her knees badly. I wanted to cry too.

Elena slipped her hand in mine, and I leaned into her as Camila's mom snapped at Alfonso to join them. Enzo came running with him, but Tony stayed on the slides. He never listened. I didn't like him or Alfonso, but they were sort of family, just with a different last name and parents. At least that was what Mom said. We were the Five Families, and that linked us together.

When Elena's fingers tightened, mine did too. I felt it. Something was wrong—not with Camila but with the men daddy had sent to watch over us. One fell. There were popping sounds.

The moms were shouting, screaming for us to come to them. Everyone was running or shooting. It was like when my brothers played war, but I knew it wasn't pretend. Elena's fingers bit into mine. I couldn't move. Things were going too fast but also too slow. Enzo grabbed my arm, jerking me with him. I pulled Elena. Alfonso was there. His mom clutched Marissa and Camila as she tried to grab Alfonso.

He was just out of reach, but not from me. So close that I could touch him. My hand lifted as his eyes went wide, his body stumbling forward into Elena and me. He jerked again and again. Red colored his shirt, splashing his neck. I screamed. Elena's hand slid from mine as Alfonso fell against her. I followed, my hands bracing my fall, and a sharp pain sliced through my palm. Then Enzo yanked me to my feet. I couldn't look away. They didn't move.

"Don't look!" Enzo shouted in my ear, turning me away with a pull so hard it made my shoulder hurt. Enzo forced me to run with him. I didn't look back.

Scary men in black with guns were everywhere. Tears streamed down my face, and my side and hand hurt. When Enzo stopped by the tunnel slide, he pushed my head down and shoved me in. My knees skidded on the plastic, and then he was behind me, his hand on the back of my leg, urging me to move.

I climbed, slipping a few times on the hem of my dress. Enzo caught me then tugged on my skirt to stop it from getting tangled under my feet and also to stop me. I turned to see his face, to make sure he was real. My body shook hard like it was cold outside, but it wasn't. My teeth chattered. I couldn't make them stop. Then his arms wrapped around me while his legs braced us in the middle of the slide, hidden from the men swarming the playground.

"You're okay," he whispered close to my ear.

I wanted to believe him, but Elena and Alfonso—the red that covered them, the vacant look in Alfonso's eyes, and my throbbing side said otherwise. When I looked down, the same color had spread over the pretty pink of my dress and down the ballerina skirt, and a sob broke free from my chattering teeth. *I want my mom.* I lifted shaky hands. I'd cut myself when I fell. Blood pooled along my palm, dripping down my wrist. I was afraid I would throw up.

I hated to throw up. Last time I was sick, I threw up five times. My head hurt, and so did my stomach. It was messy and smelled. I didn't want to do that in front of Enzo. He would think I was a baby, when all I wanted was for him to play with me as he did with the other boys. When he did, it was the best day ever. That day wasn't like that, even though we were together.

"Shh." Enzo put his finger to his lips then looked at my palm. He got that serious face of his. Brown eyes met mine, and the strength in them slowed my tears a little. He dug in his pocket and pulled out the knife he'd showed Alfonso last time we went to the park. He'd said his dad had given it to him. "I'll keep you safe. I promise."

I shook my head. "They'll come for us." I didn't know who they were, but I meant the men who'd hurt our friends. The shivering worsened. I couldn't stop it. I didn't know why, but the bad men had gone around my mom and Nicole, Tony's mom, then shot at us. We were who they wanted—the kids.

"No. I won't let them take you." He opened the pocketknife then held the tip of the blade at the palm of his hand. "You know what a blood oath is, right?"

I nodded, and the tremors lessened. Marco, my oldest brother, had once pricked the tip of my finger, squeezing it until a drop of blood showed. He'd repeated the steps with his own finger then pressed it against mine, making the blood smear together. He said it was a promise that could never be broken because we'd sworn it in blood.

What Enzo was doing felt like a big deal. I watched, fascinated as he drew the blade across his palm until he bled. Then he grabbed mine, the one that was cut open and bleeding, and pressed them together.

"I swear to protect you." His warm brown eyes were fierce, determined. And I couldn't help but be swept up in the moment as he repeated the oath my oldest brother had said to me that one time. Enzo would save me, that day and always. I knew it in my blood as it pumped and mixed with his. "I'll always be there for you, come for you, and keep you safe."

"Sofia." Eva snapped her fingers in front of my face, and as I jerked back, the past faded away and my studio came into sharp focus.

I drew in a steadying breath as the horror of that day when I was six and Enzo was eight left the forefront of my mind. We'd lost Alfonso that day. Elena had survived. They'd thought she wouldn't make it—a bullet that had pierced her side. She'd lain in a pool of Alfonso's blood with his body half on her, and they'd thought she, too, was dead.

The attack had been meant for her. The Russians wanted her dead, or so I'd overheard from my parents. But I'd never learned why. After that day, Elena's mom dyed her hair from brown with caramel highlights to black to help keep her safe. It was something they did together over the years, and I'd thought it was a cool mother-daughter-bonding thing. While it might have been, the main reason had been to make a disguise. Elena stopped going to parks, and as we grew up, she stayed close to Nicole's side, only playing with Marissa and me in our homes, rarely outside.

"Sofia." Eva grabbed my shoulder and gave me a shake.

"Sorry." I forced a half smile. "I need more coffee. What did you say?"

Eva rolled her eyes. "Is Enzo coming to Milan?"

Agitation made me itch, and I rubbed my arms. "Why would he? He's not my protector." *He's not mine. Not anymore. Even if I wish he was.*

CHAPTER TWO

SOFIA

With a sigh, I turned the sewing machine off then stood to hang the dress I'd finished altering with the others that would go to the show in Milan. Metal clicked as the hanger made contact with the rack. I would fly to Italy, where my line would debut, in a week. God, I was tired.

The sun was setting. It wasn't as late as I'd thought. At least I wasn't staying until midnight, and my oldest brother, Marco, wouldn't show up to check on me. Years before, that would have been Enzo, but everything had changed when Emiliana, his sister and one of my best friends, was taken by a guard whose loyalty had been turned by an enemy. I shivered at the thought of how horrible those months were.

I glanced around the room, making sure I'd put everything away before I called my security detail for a ride home. Satisfied, I leaned against the edge of the large bay window and swiped my phone from the seat when a woman two stories below caught my attention. She stood under the glow of the café across the street, talking to a tall man with blond hair. I would have recognized both of them anywhere.

What the hell is Eva doing with Ivan?

Hands on her hips, she said something that made his lips curve into a smirk before she turned and jogged across the street. Then his gaze traveled up the ornate limestone to where I stood, bathed in light from my studio. I sucked in a breath and jerked back, my pulse racing erratically. *Why is he here?*

I hadn't seen him since the first semester of our senior year in college. Before that, I'd caught a glimpse of him when I met with Katya, the Russian assassin, and for those few seconds, he'd seemed too interested in me. I didn't like it. Neither had Enzo. If he found out Ivan was back in town, he would stick to me like glue.

I groaned, hanging my head and letting my long dark hair curtain around my face. While I wanted Enzo around me more than anything, having Ivan as the reason would bring too much attention to Elena's secret, which I'd promised to keep.

And I would, though I hadn't considered Ivan. I sent a text to my oldest brother, Marco, because he needed to know that one of the sons of the Pavlov Bratva was watching my building. I kept Ivan in my sights as Eva hit the buzzer to come up. I checked the camera to make sure she was alone then let her in.

My phone rang as Eva burst into my studio, her cheeks tinged with red and a mischievous sparkle making her brown eyes a pretty amber. I held a finger up to quiet her.

I answered, and Marco's commanding voice shouted in my ear, "Where's Sam?"

I peeked through the glass door and spotted my head security guy's concerned face as he spoke into his communication piece, his gun unholstered and held by his thigh. "He's here. I'm good. Promise. Just thought you should know."

"Nico's close. He's on his way."

I slapped my forehead. My brothers were crazy protective, especially since I was the youngest and the only girl, something they would never let me forget. "I'm fine," I said with a smirk, injecting humor in my voice to calm him down. "You do understand the meaning of that word. And what it'll mean for you if you make a huge production out of my leaving here with more security?"

Static or rustling sounded, and my spine snapped to attention as my dad's voice took the place of my brother's.

"You listen here, baby girl. I know I didn't hear you giving your brother any lip. Your mother and I would have his head if one hair on yours was harmed."

They would too. Tears misted my eyes. I was lucky. My parents loved me more than life itself. Not all my friends had what I did.

"Do not move from your studio until both Nico and Tom escort you out and back home."

"Yes, Papa," I relented with as much grace as I could muster.

I disconnected before Marco could get back on. I would give him hell later, just because it was fun, and he deserved it.

"Are they sending in the calvary?" Eva arched a perfectly sculpted brow.

"Yeah." I was distracted as my gaze darted around and cataloged everything I would need. "Help me pack stuff up. They aren't going to let me back until they know why Ivan is here and how big of a threat he is."

"Sure." She grabbed a garment bag and started shoving everything from the rack that would fit in it inside. "Can I get a ride?"

"Of course." *How am I going to pack up everything I need for the week? And for the show? I can't leave anything.* "Why were you talking to Ivan? What did he want?"

She shrugged, her thick hair shifting over her back as she kept adding more clothes to another bag. "He didn't want anything, just made a stupid comment about Italians. Nothing serious."

"But you came over here pretty fast, and he's Russian Mafia. Come on, Eva. I need to know what he said."

She huffed then shot me an annoyed look over her shoulder. "It was nothing. He told me to come back to his room with him so he could ruin me for all men." She waved her hand then went back to what she was doing. "You know, the whole once-you-go-Russian bullshit."

"That's not even a thing." I scrunched up my nose.

"Of course it isn't. He was being a pig." Then she whirled around, that mischievous spark lighting her features again. "He is big, though."

I rolled my eyes. "Only you."

"Hey, I think I have a way for you to get out of being locked up."

I paused in gathering fabrics, interested in her idea. There was a reason I had a studio on North Michigan Avenue—to work in peace and quiet, which wasn't possible with three brothers and my parents at home, no matter how big our house was. "I'm listening."

"Let's go to the lake house. I ran into Tony before Ivan showed up. He was game and said he'd tell everyone else. Your brothers can't be mad, especially when one or two of them will probably be there."

That was true. I grinned. "If Enzo isn't going, we need to grab Emiliana." It was unlikely her brother would be able to get away because of his responsibilities as second-in-command. I knew Marco wouldn't either. But my other two brothers, Nico and Trey, would join us. They loved the lake house too.

Tom tapped on the door's glass pane with his knuckle, a signal to wrap it up. I went over and opened the door. "Can you send a few guys up to carry everything out?"

"That's not the order, Sofia." Tom leveled his stern gaze on me.

It did no good. "I won't leave without my line. You know how important this show is. Send two. You can spare at least that many to carry what Eva and I can't."

He spoke in his comm unit then motioned for us to follow him as the two guards he'd called forward went into the room. From there, things went smoothly. The guys grabbed all my bags and fabrics. Eva and I were surrounded and escorted to waiting SUVs. I glanced across the street to where I'd seen Ivan. He wasn't there, but I knew that wasn't the last I would see of him.

The rhythmic waves crashed against the shore. The lake house's tiered deck was surrounded on either side by trees that didn't obstruct the water view. Leaves rustled in the wind. It was gorgeous and peaceful. I'd dropped my bags inside and followed Trey outside immediately, breathing deeply. It was my favorite place to go in Michigan.

The house was huge, with over twenty bedrooms. It had been in my family for decades. Over the past few years, it had become a place where many of us in the Mafia families—our generation, anyway—went to have some fun away from our responsibilities.

"Thanks for convincing Mom, Dad, and Marco to let me go." I wrapped my arm my brother Trey, closest in age and closest to me in general. Trey was brilliant—a genius, really—and had breezed through medical school in a fraction of the time it would have taken anyone else. He finished high school at fifteen and was doing his residency with ease, despite the dark circles that had become a permanent fixture under his eyes. But our family worked hard. Having billions wasn't an excuse to be lazy —our parents had instilled the work ethic we all had into us at a young age.

"Best idea you've had in a long time, Sofia." He ruffled my hair, and that infectious grin that stopped women in their tracks curved his handsome face.

I leaned into him, and he wrapped an arm around me. "It was Eva's idea, but once she suggested it, I couldn't think of anything else."

I peered into the surrounding trees. They stretched for several acres in both directions and were currently filled with Mafia soldiers patrolling the grounds. "They sent enough security with us."

Trey put two fingers under my chin and tipped my face up to him, something that annoyed me. He was only a year older but still managed to tower over me. Most of the guys in our group did.

"You can't make light of this, sis." Worry clouded his amber eyes. "Ivan isn't someone to take lightly. The fact that Mom and Dad let you come here is nothing short of a miracle."

"It's because you and Nico came with. I get that, but what's going to happen when I fly to Italy next week? I can't cancel. It's my first show. I have to be there for that one. Besides, Ivan is here. And why would he follow me?"

"Why indeed?" He raised one of his brows, too smart for his own good.

"You know nothing." I smacked his flat stomach, rolled my eyes, then sucked in a breath as my peripheral vision caught a glimpse of Enzo as he strolled onto the deck not far from where we stood. My body stiffened, and a deep longing filled me.

Trey sighed. "I don't know what happened between you two. You were so close. He came back different after Emiliana's abduction."

"I know. She did too." It had happened right before we'd started college four years before, and she didn't join us right away, needing time to heal and recover from a horrible experience I wouldn't have wished on my worst enemy. "But his withdrawal sucks."

Trey squeezed my shoulders as Eva burst from the French

doors on the back of the house, a bag of marshmallows in one hand and skewers in the other.

I grinned at the sight of Lil's carefree party cousin. All my tension eased as I spotted Emiliana not far behind Eva. She wore a fitted red T-shirt, a color that highlighted her long almost-black hair, olive skin, and almond-shaped eyes framed in spikey lashes. She was gorgeous and lethal, and the bastards who'd taken her hadn't managed to destroy her either. "Gotta go." I winked at Trey, pushing his arm from my shoulders as I hugged Em.

The sun was getting ready to set, and more people trickled in. There had to have been an army of Mafia soldiers between the different families with all of us in one place, but we had more than enough space inside and the two guesthouses where the guards could go when they had breaks from their shifts. Tom hadn't been pleased about the trip but seemed to worry less when he heard my brothers and Enzo would be joining us. I hadn't mentioned Tony, as I secretly hoped he wouldn't show.

Lil, Em, and I had sworn that Tony was the one responsible for Marissa's death. After we held him hostage and questioned him, we couldn't make the connection between her murder and him. But none of us liked him. Good thing he wasn't second-in-command anymore, since Max had taken over the Caruso family and stripped Tony of most of his power.

But he did turn up at the lake house, and I locked eyes on the hard glint in Tony's over Em's shoulder while I hugged her. He hadn't fully forgiven us for tying him up when Lil was taken hostage by his now dead father, Antonio. "Wish Lil was here too," I murmured for only Em's ears.

She squeezed my hand then followed my gaze to where Tony sat next to Eva. The fire pit had wood stacked in it, and someone had lit it. "Me too, but I bet she's having an amazing time with Max. Did she say if she'd be at the show in Milan?"

"Yes." Warmth filled me that Lil would be there, even if she was on her honeymoon with Max. They'd waited for weeks to get away after their wedding and deserved the time alone. "But they're flying back right after. And you'll be there for the next one." I flashed her a bright smile. Traveling to Italy wasn't high on Em's list. It'd been only four years since she was there last, under nightmarish circumstances.

A jerky nod was her only response, and I hurried to change the subject. "I'm surprised Tony showed up. Although"—I tilted my head to the side, scrutinizing how close he was to Eva, their faces inches apart—"if I didn't know any better, I would swear something was going on between those two."

"We should find out." She tugged me toward the fire pit.

Neither of us trusted Tony, even though we'd known him all our lives. After Max's return from the dead—which shocked the hell out of all of us—Tony had been bumped from the position of Antonio's underboss to nothing. From what Lil had told us, Max wasn't sure if Tony would make a good leader in the family and hadn't yet figured out where his place would be.

Tony was the equivalent of a gold digger but for power. He craved it, although he wasn't the best at wielding it. In his eyes, Lil should have been his, along with the Brambilla Mafia arm of the Five Families. If he had married her, he would have eventually taken over as boss. With Max as boss of the Caruso family, Tony had nothing, and that made him desperate and dangerous.

"We need to watch him." Em's whisper echoed my own thoughts.

"Agreed," I murmured as we took seats near Eva around the fire.

Eva handed out two glasses from a tray on the table behind her. "I thought we could do vodka and lemonade tonight rather than wine."

I shrugged. "Sure." I was glad it was unseasonably warm for September as my gaze followed Enzo. He glanced back at me, and the air crackled with the intensity of his predatory gaze. Snared in his sight, my body heated. I had to force myself to stay where I was as he joined my brothers. They made their way down to the beach, stripping off their shirts but leaving their guns tucked into the waistbands of their swim trunks. Visually, I traced every sinewy line of muscle along Enzo's back as he flexed, imagining my fingers running over them. *Yeah, I could use something stronger too.*

Tony took one look at us then got to his feet and headed to follow the rest of the guys. Enzo probably wasn't his favorite, either, but he didn't have anything against Nico or Trey, at least not as far as I knew.

"So, Eva." Em moved to sit across from her then leaned forward. Her long hair slipped over her shoulders and framed her face. "What's the deal with you and Tony?"

Eva's hand stilled, the pitcher of vodka and lemonade hovering in the air before she recovered and set it down. "I don't know what you're talking about."

"Please." I nudged Eva's shoulder. "There was a moment between you, a very heated one where you got lost in his eyes. We both saw it."

She shrugged. "What does it matter? He won't marry beneath him. He wants a boss's daughter and the connection it will afford him."

"He thinks he has a right to be boss," Em said. "That didn't work out all that well for him with Liliana. Max took what he thought would be his. There is no one else in the Five Families to marry that would gain him that kind of power."

"Yep." A sad smile curved Eva's lips. "Marco will lead Sofia's family. Enzo yours." She waved at Emiliana. "And Stefano is the eldest and only son of Frank Rossi."

"Then what's stopping the two of you from getting togeth- er?" I hated seeing the pain in her eyes.

"I'm only a cousin. He won't gain any favor if we were

together. I don't know what he's thinking or wants to do. But it doesn't seem like it will ever be with me."

Ivan and the Pavlov Bratva, with its structure that was eerily similar to the Italian Mafia, flashed before me. *Will Tony turn outside the families and try to establish a position in one of the Russian ones? Will they even accept him? Doubtful.*

Eva turned to me, her gaze narrowed, and my thoughts scattered to the wind. "And what about you and Enzo? You couldn't take your eyes off him."

Pain flashed over Em's face almost too quickly to see, but I did. It wasn't her fault that he'd come back different. He had, and that was that. Besides, he wasn't mine. "We both want what we can't have." I tipped my glass so that it clinked with Eva's. "At least we can drink to that."

CHAPTER THREE

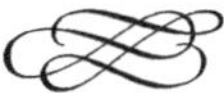

ENZO

Sofia, Lil, Emiliana, and Eva were in the lake house's backyard with enough guards patrolling the grounds to stop an army from reaching them. Sofia was the first person I saw when I stepped onto the deck. She had always been gorgeous and with way too much sass, but everything about her, from her kindness to her bravery to the way her touch felt, made me complete. I'd always been drawn to her, even when we were young. If only my dad hadn't agreed to the arranged marriage with Frank Rossi's adopted daughter, Elena. There had been things left unsettled between him and Frank, and I'd paid the price and lost my shot at Sofia, the girl of my dreams.

Elena had gone missing around the same time my sister had. We'd found her DNA among the rubble where they'd kept her and the other abducted and abused girls. The explosion and fire had burned all but one section of the back of the house—where hers and a few of the others' clothes were. She'd been there. There was no reason to suspect she was still alive because we ran that human trafficking cell into the ground, destroying them all.

With Elena gone, there was no contract to uphold. I was free to marry whomever I chose. It would have been Sofia, if I could ensure nothing like what happened to my sister would ever happen to her, but I couldn't. Emiliana hadn't been safe. She'd been targeted, and I couldn't shake the fear that anyone close to me would be, too, as both had suffered. I would do anything to keep Sofia safe—even if it was from me.

Sofia's laugh drew my gaze again. The sound, infectious and full of mischief and joy, had snared me even when we were young. I couldn't look away from her, but I was too angry to have a rational conversation. Rage had built ever since I'd spoken to Marco the night before about the threat from the Russian Bratva. Her brother thought Ivan had his sights on Sofia. We weren't positive why, but Marco and I both agreed that I would make sure nothing happened to her while she was in Milan.

⸻

Sofia

Two drinks in, I felt him. Every nerve ending in my body went on alert, my back arched slightly, and my breathing quickened. Enzo had always had that effect on me. There was no point in turning to confirm that he was behind me. I already knew he was.

There was a time when he would gravitate to my side, joke with me, throw his arm around me, and pull me against him. Even though he'd kept his distance because of the pending arranged marriage to Elena, we were close. They thought she was dead, and even with the contract null and void under their assumptions, he'd remained distant. It broke my heart, and I wished I could confide in him, but I couldn't.

"Sofia."

The caress of his deep voice sent a volley of goose bumps over my skin. The sun was setting, and I sat around the fire with Emiliana, Eva, Tony, and my brothers, who had joined us. Banking on the fading light to hide the hope in my eyes that I couldn't for the life of me kill, I turned around then looked up. He loomed over me, all six foot two of him.

"Enzo." I couldn't help it. He was being dramatic, and I childishly mocked him on the off chance that it would camouflage my reaction to his presence.

The light from the fire danced over his chiseled features, highlighting how devastatingly handsome he was. He jerked his head in the direction of the beach, where the sun was blazing a fiery trail as it descended below the horizon. Guess he didn't think I was as funny as I did.

"Go for a walk with me." He offered his hand to help me up.

His larger palm engulfed mine in warmth as he effortlessly pulled me to my feet. I maintained a tight grip on my drink. Something told me I would need it until he plucked the fortifying beverage from my fingers and set it on a nearby table, causing me to mumble "control freak" under my breath.

An amused smile curved his kissable lips as he rested one of those big hands at the small of my back and propelled me away from the group. Silence settled around us as we picked our way through the yard until it gave way to more sand than grass then only sand. I kicked off my shoes, and he maneuvered me until he caged me in with him on one side and the breaking waves on the other.

I let the area's peacefulness surround me, wishing that our circumstances were different but not knowing what I could do to change them. The heat from his body kept the chilly evening air at bay. I waited for him to talk about whatever was bothering him—and there was something, because he practically vibrated with anger. It could have been a couple of things: Italy, Ivan.

We walked for a while until he seemed calm enough to speak. At least that was the read I got off him. I braced myself regardless. If he even thought to tell me I couldn't go to Italy, he was in for one hell of an argument. He wasn't my father, brother, or husband. Even if he was—well, I had to listen to my father and Marco, but that was it.

He cleared his throat, and the fine hairs along my arms stood at attention. "Tell me about Ivan Pavlov."

I stubbed my toe on a rock and winced, pausing to catch my breath from the sharp stab of pain. Enzo wrapped his arm around me, pulling me close while I waited for it to turn to a dull ache then go away. He started to bend to look at it, but I snapped that I was fine. I needed to finish the conversation. We resumed our walk, and I spit out what I could about Ivan. "I'm sure I know the same as you. He was at school for one semester, the one before Marissa was killed. Then he disappeared."

"And you still think Tony killed Marissa?"

I could feel the weight of his mocking stare but refused to meet his gaze. "I don't know." It made more sense than Ivan did, and I was a tad embarrassed I'd accused Tony. But ugh, that guy rubbed me the wrong way and had since we were little. He was too much like his father but without discipline and drive.

"Why is Ivan singling you out?"

I was pressed against his side as we strolled along the packed sand, the waves occasionally rolling over our toes in a back-and-forth dance. The feel of his body made it hard to think. I wanted to turn in his arms then feel his lips expertly move over mine. *If only he would.* Mentally, I sighed. He was giving me mixed signals —a look, a touch, but then so much distance. But our walk wasn't about his interest or lack thereof in me. It was a fact-finding mission. "Your guess is as good as mine as to why Ivan was across the street from my studio. Maybe it was coincidence."

"You know better than that." His fingers dipped so that he

was holding my hip instead of my waist. "Eva told Tony that when she turned around to go into the building, Ivan was staring at your window."

"So? That doesn't mean anything. He could have seen movement and looked up. Who knows? Besides, it doesn't matter. I leave for Italy soon. Ivan is here."

"About that. Trey and Nico were talking about going with you to Milan."

The tension in my shoulders lessened. "That sounds fair." My brothers took my safety seriously, but they would be interested in other pursuits. There would be plenty of women to distract them when they thought I was safe and secure in my room with our guards.

"I volunteered to go instead."

"What?" I broke free from his grasp and faced him. That wasn't a good idea. Way too much temptation when I knew the reason behind why I couldn't act on the desire that was always just beneath the surface for him. "Why?"

"Why would I want to go with you?" That mischievous grin that I loved curved his lips. "I'm not letting you out of my sight for even a second the entire time you're there. I know your brothers. You would have free, unsupervised time without them meaning to give it to you."

Panic laced my blood. I could barely resist him on a normal basis. *What the heck am I going to do if we share a suite? Or when he's by my side every minute for a solid week? I shouldn't do this, but...* "What about Emiliana? Are you going to leave your sister here while Ivan is in town?"

The grin fell away, and a muscle along the side of his jaw pulsed. "No. Ivan wasn't anywhere near her, and Stefano will be keeping an eye on her."

This is bad. I needed to talk to Katya, but I wasn't sure the Russian assassin was around. We'd only spoken a handful of times since the summer before college. If anyone could have kept Ivan in check, it was her. "No."

"No?" He took a step closer, only a handful of inches separating us. "It's already done. I put in a call to your father before I even thought to talk to you about what would happen."

I rammed my finger into his chest, leaning forward even more. "You had no right." His hand curled around my wrist, and I pushed up on my toes, intent on giving him a taste as to why the two of us alone were a bad idea. My gaze dropped to his lips, and then my mouth was on his in a soft caress.

With a growl, Enzo released my wrist to wrap his arm around my waist, holding me tightly against his body as his lips crashed down on mine. With one hand, he threaded his fingers through my hair, cupping the back of my head as he angled it then deepened the kiss.

I melted into him as his tongue danced with mine. My body was on fire. I gripped his shoulders, fingers digging into the solid strength as I held on while everything around us faded. There was only him and the way he was kissing me as if I was his next breath after being suspended underwater for too long.

When he drew back, my head spun. I would have fallen if he hadn't been holding me up. I wanted more than anything to forget what I knew, to let it happen between us. But I couldn't. "That's why you can't go with me, Enzo." Sadness coated my voice, conveying the longing that resided deep in my soul, where it would have to remain. When he gave me a nod, my heart fractured because there wasn't anything more he was offering. I knew it, and so did he.

He loosened his hold but kept his hands on my hips. "I want this. What's always been between us. You have to know that, Sofia."

Tears misted my eyes, but I refused to let them fall. "Yeah. I do."

"They took my sister. What's stopping them from an attempt

on my wife? I can't let anything happen. *Not to you.* You have to know that, to understand after all these years what you mean to me. I swore a blood oath to protect you, even if it's from myself. I'm barely holding on after what happened to my sister. I won't survive the same thing or worse being done to you."

CHAPTER FOUR

SOFIA

I needed answers, and they weren't to be found at the lake house. Things between Enzo and me were still as messed up as ever. Once we'd returned from our walk on the beach, I sat next to Emiliana by the fire pit. She'd taken one look at my swollen lips and sad eyes then wrapped me in a hug.

The fiery kiss between Enzo and I had notes of finality in it, and my heart broke all over again. Whether Elena wanted to marry him or not didn't matter. An arranged marriage contract in the Mafia wasn't something one could just break. There were consequences. And while I knew it was in effect because she was alive, Enzo did not. The fact that he thought he was free and still wouldn't choose me killed me.

I hadn't stayed long on Sunday except to hang with Em and Eva on the beach. In the late afternoon, I made my brothers pack up, and we headed home. I had a few things left to do to prepare for Milan, and I wanted to put as much distance between Enzo and me as I could until forced to be in his presence in Italy.

My nerves were frayed. Lil had even called on her honeymoon. It was great to hear her voice, but I hated the reason for her call. Max found out about Ivan from Stefano, and she was freaking out. I promised I was fine and relayed details about the round-the-clock security I had. It was a surprise I could even go to the bathroom without someone following me.

Fast forward to Monday, and I felt like a caged animal in my house. I couldn't go anywhere without a shadow—one of my brothers—and double my usual guard. And that morning, I had *someone* I needed to talk to without anyone knowing.

Door locked and phone in hand, I scrolled through my contacts for Katya. I shot off a text asking if she was in town and if she could meet. Not even a second later, I got a reply: *Fifteen minutes, The Coffee Stop.* It was near my house. I just had to talk one of my brothers into going with me. Trey was the obvious answer. He thought the barista was hot, and that would work in my favor.

I shoved my phone into the tight pocket of my jeans, threw my dark-brown hair into a high ponytail, and grabbed my sunglasses. I was ready. I weaved through the halls to his room then pounded on the door.

"What the hell?" He whipped open the door, his dark hair sticking up in all directions. He was still in pajama pants slung low on his hips. If Eva had been there, she would have had to wipe the drool from the corner of her lips. I wasn't oblivious. My brothers were hot. But ew, they were my brothers.

"You're taking me to The Coffee Stop. Throw on jeans and run your fingers through your hair. I want to leave in two minutes." He grumbled as I turned my back on him. He was going back to bed. I knew it. "Teresa is working this morning."

I peeked over my shoulder to see him deviate from the bed to where he'd tossed his jeans last night. Sucker. I had no idea if Teresa was working, but I knew he was more than interested in her. If he hadn't been so crazy busy with his residency, he would've asked her out already. Maybe he would.

Ten minutes later, I was snapping at Trey to hurry the hell

up. I was five minutes late and worried Katya wouldn't wait for me. When we were in front of the coffee place, I couldn't help the grin at the tagline beneath the store's name: a socially acceptable chemical dependence. They'd gotten that right. I was a coffee addict.

The bell jingled overhead as we walked through and into the welcoming interior, another thing I loved about the place. The atmosphere was perfect with soft lighting, exposed brick, dark wood, metal furniture, and many plants. Some sections offered privacy, at least enough for the patrons who wanted to enjoy their drink and not feel like they were out in the open for all the other paying customers to see.

I caught a flash of blond hair to my left and shoved Trey toward the counter. "Get me my usual. I see a friend I want to talk to."

Trey scowled at me until Teresa came from the back room and resumed her place at the cash register, effectively distracting my brother. I suppressed a grin so he wouldn't argue with me and edged away from him. When he continued forward, no doubt sure that the guards stationed outside would keep me safe, I pivoted on my heel and hurried over to the secluded table surrounded by tall, leafy plants.

"You shouldn't be out." I could barely hear Katya's accent in her hushed words.

I met her blue eyes with a determined glare. "Why? I'm not reckless. Trey is here, and I have a massive number of guards trailing my every move. What is going on? Why is Ivan here? Because it feels personal, that his goal is me."

"We don't know why he's here." Katya leaned back in her seat. She had no other tells. Her blue gaze was unwavering. She existed in stillness. "I can guess."

I frowned at the Russian assassin. "And your guess is?" I had to ask, but in my heart, I thought I knew—Elena.

After Elena's mom died, Nicole and Antonio Caruso took

Elena into their house as an adopted daughter at a very young age. Enzo and Elena's arranged marriage had been put in place for her protection—the Russians had targeted her during the shoot-out in the park when I was six.

Katya's lips curved on one side in a half grin. "We both know it must be because of Elena. His spies must have learned something, passed the information on to him." She leaned forward, and her hand clamped on my wrist, holding it in place before I could even react. My heart sped, but I refused to show fear.

"I'm here to keep an eye on him until I'm called back to Russia. Fair warning, it'll be soon. Be smart." Her voice remained low so the sound would not carry. "Ivan isn't someone you want to tangle with. He likes to break girls." Her gaze narrowed. "Prove me right. I picked you to help for a reason— you're tougher than you look."

I refused to comment on that last part. I was small. I got it. But no one would get the drop on me without one hell of a fight. My brothers had made sure I was well versed in hand-to-hand combat as well as weapons training. They were relentless, tough, and thorough. If for any reason Ivan did manage to corner me and—God forbid—try to get information by using his awful brand of torture, I wouldn't crack. Elena's location would remain safe.

Still, I didn't like how Katya had worded things. "When you say 'we,' who do you mean? And why are you helping me?"

In a fluid motion, she got to her feet. "I'm not here to piece things together for you. That's not my job. My orders are only to watch Ivan and to intervene if he makes a move on you or any of those I'm told to protect, and that's only while I'm here." She turned, but before she left, she delivered one more piece of advice over her shoulder. "I'm aware of your show. Do not go alone. Bring an army."

Chills skated over my skin as Katya slipped away, and then I was yanked hard behind Trey, who had his gun drawn. The scent of cinnamon latte was strong, and my anger bubbled up. "Dammit, Trey! Did you spill my coffee?"

He rounded on me, a mixture of fury and fear swimming in his eyes, evident in the clenched jaw and twitching muscle along it. "Care to tell me why you were talking to Katya?" He clamped his hand tightly on my upper arm.

I opened my mouth to argue when the door to The Coffee Stop slammed against the back wall. My gaze whipped to who had entered, and another wave of pure irritation shot through me. "Why are you here?"

Enzo stalked over, removed Trey's hand, then used his sheer hulking size to back me against the brick wall between the plants. He rested a palm over my head and leaned in.

I shoved at his chest, my pent-up anger at how annoying both Trey and he were being growing. "Back off, Enzo."

"I can't trust you alone for a second. Trouble seems to find you wherever you go."

"I'm not alone. Trey is with me, and there *is no trouble!*" God, I was surrounded by testosterone. "I'm not in any danger from Katya. She's sort of a friend."

"She's a Russian assassin. We've had this discussion before," Enzo growled, his face inches from mine. "Even if you think she's on your side, she's not. She could turn on you too quickly for you to react, slitting your pretty throat like butter before you even know what happened. Knives are her specialty. Did you know that? Ever see her handiwork?"

I shook my head, fuming. He had no idea, and the fact that I couldn't tell him bothered me more than I could let on. "I'm not in danger from her."

"How do you know her? The truth this time, Sof." A flicker of something entered his dark eyes, and his tongue swiped across his bottom lip, drawing my focus. Victory sparked through me at the telltale sign. He was thinking about our kiss.

I relaxed my hands that had been attempting to push him

away and softened my features. "I met her in college." I slid my hands from his well-defined chest up to hook behind his neck. No words were needed. I let my body do the talking for me, distracting him from his goal of intimidation and information gathering. As fluidly as I could, I eased away from the wall behind me and closed the distance between our bodies. When my chest came into contact with his solid one, air hissed from his mouth.

Our lips were centimeters from touching, and I couldn't wait for the kiss that would follow. Then a slow clap to the side snapped us apart, and I scowled at Trey.

"I can't leave you two alone for a second." Laughter surrounded us as my brother snickered. "When you dragged me here to feed your addiction, I thought you meant coffee, not Enzo."

"You little shit!" I jolted forward, hand extended to smack the crap out of him when Enzo's steel arm wound around me, holding me back. "You're lucky he's here to stop me." My gaze narrowed as I pointed my finger at him. "But he won't be around to protect you when we're home."

Trey snickered. "I'm shaking, Sof, so scared about the damage you'll do with your little hands."

I crossed my arms over my chest. "You're no longer my favorite brother."

He got up from his chair as Teresa deposited two new to-go coffees in front of him. The smile he gifted her caused her to blush from her neck to her pretty face. Trey leaned close to her and whispered a few words we couldn't hear before she giggled then turned to do her job.

Enzo backed up a step, and I felt the loss immediately, but there wasn't a thing I could do about it. "Try not to get into any more trouble, Sof. Please." His quiet plea shot guilt through me. All I could do was nod. Then he turned on his heel and went to the counter to order his coffee.

Trey said goodbye to him then handed me a coffee. He pulled me to his side, farther from the counter where Enzo stood, and wrapped his arm around my shoulders as we headed to the door to leave.

"You know I love you, sis." All the levity fled from his expression. "I couldn't live with myself if anything happened to you. Stop fighting us on protecting you."

Leaning my head on his chest, I sighed. "I know. I love you guys, too, even though you totally kiss-blocked me."

We left The Coffee Stop with Trey's laughter drowning out the bell that jingled overhead. A few of the guards closed in around us. As we got into Trey's Maserati, I couldn't help but try to steal one last glance at Enzo before we left. My fingers pressed against my lips, longing for the tangible loss of our almost kiss. In a matter of days, we would be in Italy together, and I wondered how his self-control would be there and whether I would even want him to have any.

I resigned myself to the fact that it would be like that until Ivan was back in Russia, where he belonged.

CHAPTER FIVE

ENZO

The need to chase after Sofia and glue her to my side raged through me. Instead of giving in, I let Trey lead her out of The Coffee Stop while placing an order for a drink loaded with caffeine that would not help my situation. But it gave them time to leave and for me to attempt to control my reaction to seeing her with Katya.

I barely registered getting my coffee, walking out the door, or driving home. Trey texted that Sofia was home and that Marco and their father, Robert, were up to speed with what had gone down. I had no doubt Sofia was behind Katya showing up. Keeping trouble from her was a full-time job. Thankfully, she had three brothers and me to make sure she stayed safe.

Back home, I set the to-go cup on my desk. I couldn't sit still and paced back and forth until a soft knock on my door alerted me to my sister's presence. I grabbed the drink and pasted a smile that I hoped looked genuine on my face. "I got you a coffee."

Emiliana's lips curved into a smile that didn't quite reach her eyes. The sadness that always lurked in the deep brown depths echoed what I felt in my heart with every passing minute about the hell she'd endured four years ago. I would never get over the horror of those weeks.

Outwardly, Em's appearance was unchanged unless one studied the expression in her eyes and how she preferred to fade into the background when she could. She'd been compared to a siren. Her long dark hair fell just below mid back, her lips were full, and long, spiky lashes framed her almond-shaped eyes. I knew what men saw when they looked at my sister, and I would gut every last one of them if they dared upset her in any way.

Aside from our father, there was only one other man I trusted with her—Stefano. Two if I counted Max because he was infatuated with Liliana.

"I know what happened this morning." Em's voice broke into my violent thoughts.

Of course she did. "Sofia called you?" At her nod, another wash of anger spread through me. "Was that before or after she contacted Katya to meet her at The Coffee Stop?"

Em's lips quirked up. She clearly enjoyed my frustration. "After. You don't have to worry that I was involved. I haven't seen Katya in… a while."

I narrowed my eyes. She was lying. "When was the last time, Em?"

She lifted a slender shoulder then let it fall before taking a sip of coffee. "This is good. Thanks."

"Em," I growled, impatient for her to answer my question. I crossed my arms over my chest, and she rolled her eyes. My tension eased slightly at the familiar expression.

"I haven't spoken to Katya since sometime in college. Probably in the last year, but I can't remember. I saw her not too long ago, talking with Sofia when we met for lunch, but Katya didn't stop by to say hi, just nodded to us in acknowledgment." She placed her free hand on my fore-arm. "I'm not in any danger. I have never been from her.

Neither is Sofia. Trust her if she says she's okay around Katya."

"And Ivan?"

Em pursed her lips, and the concern I felt was reflected on her face. "I would worry about him."

I ground my teeth in frustration. "Do you have any idea why he's interested in her?"

She shook her head in a slow side-to-side motion. "No. It worries me too." When she turned to go, she paused by the door then faced me once more. "Don't leave her side in Italy."

I grinned. My sister might have been more reserved after what had happened to her, but she didn't stick her head in the sand. "Who told you?"

She winked. "Who do you think?"

"I'd say Sofia." I guessed because there was something else in the sparkle in her eyes that told me all I needed to know. "But she wasn't the only one, was she?"

"Ah, dear brother"—Em leaned against the doorframe—"before we get into that, I think we should talk about why you won't date Sofia." Her voice lowered, and a shared understanding gentled what she said next. "You've always loved her. With Elena gone, what's holding you back?"

I eased back against the desk, unhappy with the turn our conversation had taken but refusing to brush her off. "You know why." My tone matched hers. "She would be more of a target with me."

"How is guarding her any different? You'll be seen around her. It'll be assumed that you care."

I ran my hand over my forehead, feeling as if I'd aged ten years. "I know, but I can't figure out any other way. If she goes with Nico and a contingent of guards, including more that I would send, I wouldn't be able to live with myself if something happened and I wasn't there to stop it." I *should* have stayed away, but I couldn't. When I lifted my gaze to hers, I almost broke down and told her that I feared I was the cause of why she had been taken.

"It wasn't your fault, Enzo." She stepped farther into the room. "If it wasn't me, it would have been Lil or Sofia. What happened had nothing to do with you. There are always risks because of the blood running through our veins. It wasn't isolated to you and me. Remember Elena lost her life in one of those human trafficking rings too. Look to the bosses and see what deal went wrong or who made a powerful enemy. Have you ventured down that avenue?"

"Not enough. With Dad, sure, but I've never felt like Antonio shared everything. I'll dig deeper. We both know he would have sold the souls of his children to the highest bidder if it got him what he wanted." He'd proven how coldhearted he was when he left his son, Max, in Italy years ago.

"Yeah, and now that he's dead, it'll be harder to find out what he was in to." She took another sip of coffee then tilted her head. "I bet Nicole would have answers. Have you talked with her? I could."

Nicole Caruso, Antonio's widow, was sharp and had managed to ferret many family secrets. "I did, but at the time, she was so grief-stricken over Elena that I backed off. Now that Ivan is back, I'll go talk to her."

"Good plan." She pivoted to leave.

"Emiliana."

At her name, she stopped.

"You brought up Sofia. It's only fair that I do the same with Stefano. What's going on there?"

A sad smile curved her lips before she faced forward again and walked through the doorway, her words floating over her shoulder. "Absolutely nothing."

Several minutes passed before I pushed away from the desk to go after her. We needed to have the conversation. It'd been four years, and I knew how deep her feelings ran for Stefano and that he wouldn't make a move on her unless she initiated it. That was the only reason why I was okay with watching him suffer in her presence. I'd seen him in action when we went after those who had taken her. There was nothing he wouldn't do to keep her safe.

I was at the bottom of the back staircase closest to Emiliana's room when my phone rang. I pulled it from my pocket to see Renato's name on the screen—Ren was our captain, the one in charge of all our soldiers. I answered right away.

"I have a tip on where Ivan is," he said.

"Where?" I shifted from the staircase to go out the back, where I'd left the car.

"He was on Michigan Avenue not far from Sofia's studio, having breakfast at one of the outdoor cafes."

I was immensely grateful to Robert La Rosa for insisting his daughter not return to her studio until the Russian was gone. We needed answers as to why he was around and toying with Sofia. "I'm heading out. Meet me there with two soldiers." I concluded my call with Ren and continued through the house to convene with him when I was intercepted by Dad.

"Enzo." Dad's commanding voice stopped me in my tracks. "Ren told me he found Ivan. Don't do anything foolish."

My hand stilled on the doorknob. I turned to look at an older version of myself. I'd inherited his square jaw, height, and wide shoulders. Em took after Mom, but she'd gotten her almost-black eyes from Dad. I had Mom's lighter amber ones, something that annoyed my sister to no end. "If Em or Mom was shadowed by Ivan, you would stop at nothing short of war with the Russians to keep them safe."

"You're right. I'm just telling you to think before you act."

"Noted." I slammed out of the house, not waiting for more advice. I hopped into the car and peeled out of there. I'd promised to proceed with caution, but when it came to Sofia, I saw red. She'd owned me from when we were little. None of my feelings for her had changed. What kept me from acting on them was fear for her safety.

I took the ramp to the highway then pushed the pedal to the floor, flying by two cops who weren't stupid enough to pursue me. Twenty minutes later, I was double-parked in front of the restaurant, Ivan's white-blond head a beacon at the four-top where he sat.

The staff took one look at me and gave me a wide berth. We owned that town. There wasn't a single person there who didn't know what we did and what would happen to them if they attempted to defy us.

I wove through the tables until I stood directly in front of him, gun still in the waistband of my pants. More than anything, I wanted to pull it on him and ram the barrel into his mouth, but I needed answers first.

He wasn't stupid enough to pretend I wasn't there. I slapped a hand on the top of his table, rattling the plate with the half-finished omelet and silverware. My eyes met his light-blue ones with the promise of violence. "Why are you here? What do you want with Sofia?"

A mocking smile curved his wide mouth. "The fact that you don't know what would draw me to her is highly amusing."

I curled my fingers in the fabric of his shirt, yanking him to his feet. My fist met the side of his face before I even knew what I was going to do.

Ivan stumbled back once I released my hold on him. Blood trickled from the corner of his mouth. With his thumb, he swiped it away then glanced at it with a sinister laugh. "She means something to you. That makes what I'm going to do so much more amusing."

"We can do this right now." My gun was in my hand, and I spread my arms wide. Screams from the patrons around us registered in the back of my mind but not enough for me to stop.

"You can't kill me. No matter how much you want to. Not even when I take her from you." Something dark passed through his eyes, ratcheting up the alarm, already fueling the adrenaline running through my body. "If you retaliate, you'll start a war."

Sofia is worth starting a war over.

CHAPTER SIX

SOFIA

I'd about fallen off the kitchen's barstool when Enzo called me with "I need your help," the sexiest words I'd heard him speak in a long time. I was still sighing over them as Emiliana and I pulled up in front of Nicole Caruso's mansion. They had a nice ring to them.

So much had happened in the last couple of weeks, big changes to one of the branches of our Mafia families. Newly widowed from Antonio Caruso, Max's dad, Nicole had been set free but allowed to maintain a vast fortune and the house she'd lived in with her former husband.

We hadn't come alone. Enzo had wanted to talk to her himself, but Emiliana and I thought we could get more information than he could. Finally, he'd agreed, but not without the ten guards he'd sent on top of my shadow of eight soldiers, including Tom, our family's captain. To have said that he and my family were paranoid would have been a generous assessment. Aside from the sheer obnoxiousness of our entourage, I found Enzo's protectiveness sweet, reminiscent of how he'd always treated me.

The other requirement to leave the house was that I took the

Mercedes, as it was basically an armored car. I was good with that. It was fun to drive and fit my mood.

Em was silent in the passenger seat, and I wished more than anything that Lil was with us. Revisiting any portion of the time when Em was abducted would have been hard for her, and the three of us together were solid—plus, it would have been added support for Em. I got that she was struggling with what we would talk to Nicole about. Asking about Elena and the connections Antonio had to the Russians would only bring back bad memories for Em, and I wanted to do anything to help her through it.

A violent killing spree might have helped her, but we weren't currently at war, despite the warning Benito had given Lil that one was coming a few weeks ago. She'd thought he'd meant between her family and the cartel, but I wondered if he was the one stirring up issues with the Russians. Guess we'd find out soon enough.

"Are you all right?" I squeezed Em's hand before making a move to get out of the car. She turned to me, and I struggled to hold in the gasp at the naked pain in her eyes.

"It's difficult. Talking to Nicole about that time brings everything back to the forefront like it was yesterday." She shivered. "I can taste the fear and humiliation. It makes me want to shoot anything that moves."

In her right hand, she had a death grip on her gun. It rested against her thigh, but I knew she wouldn't hesitate if she needed to use it. We both wore the pants that I'd designed explicitly for Lil, Em, Eva, and me. There were weapons hidden in pockets that weren't visible to the casual observer or anyone who didn't know they were there—many knives. A choke wire was sewn into the seam and accessible by the decorative metal, a one-inch bar at the hip. Pulling that made the wire emerge with ease.

I gentled my voice. "Why are you doing this, Em?" A surge of anger tore through me. "Why is Enzo letting you?" That at least brought a small smile to her face.

"Because I insisted on going. The only reason why he gave in is that he's here, too, somewhere." Of course he was. Lately, I felt like I couldn't sneeze without him emerging from the shadows to make sure I was okay. "Still. He's got to know this brings the monsters out of that locked mental box you keep them in."

"Know about that, huh?"

"We've all got monsters. Some are just stronger, more deadly than others. Take Lil, for example. She lived with one all her life."

Em blew out a breath then shifted her gaze to the mansion. "Let's do this."

That was my cue to get out. I scrambled out of the car and hurried to her side as she closed the door, her gun still clutched in her hand. I didn't know how Nicole would react to that, but some part of me thought she would understand. Elena wasn't her natural-born daughter, but those two had been closer than most mothers and daughters I knew.

Tom stood to the side of the door, waiting. We couldn't even go in without the captain shadowing us. I wanted to roll my eyes, but I got it. At least I was out of the house. I had to appreciate the little things. And they hadn't forced me to cancel Milan —I could still attend Fashion Week, where I would launch my career.

It didn't take long until the staff ushered us inside and to the formal sitting room, where Nicole sat with a magazine in hand. Her neatly fashioned shoulder-length blond hair was secured at the nape of her neck, where a strand of pearls was fastened. Out of habit, I appraised her chic pantsuit. *Chanel. Nice.* We entered, and a smile spread across her plastic-looking face—the surgeries had made her appear way too young. She'd had too much work done. I wondered if she would stop since she didn't have to please Antonio anymore.

"Girls, what a wonderful surprise!" Her gaze dropped to Emiliana's gun pointed at the ground before she gave us both hugs. "Is everything okay?"

I shrugged, and Em offered a halfhearted grimace. Better to rip the Band-Aid off. "I'm sorry to do this, to bring up painful memories, but I need to ask you some questions."

Understanding shone in her eyes. Nicole was intelligent. She picked up on cues immediately. The gun in Em's hand had to have made sense all of a sudden.

We all sat. Emiliana settled on my left and Nicole on the opposite love seat, the coffee table between us. "Something's going on, and we're in the dark, which you know is a dangerous thing. Ivan Pavlov is in town and showing a little too much interest in me. We have no idea if he was sent here by his father or if he's acting on his own."

"And you think he was somehow connected to what happened when Elena and Emiliana were taken?" Her voice cracked. She sucked in a breath and waited for a few beats while a struggle for control played through her hard eyes. "I can't say that he was, but I don't know everything Antonio did. The only thing I can give you is that he was agitated around that time. He knew something was happening, and there were many meetings with Frank Rossi."

Emiliana sucked in a breath, and I physically felt her pain. If Frank had betrayed her, it was possible that his son Stefano had known beforehand. I turned to Em and grabbed her arm. "You know better."

"I do." She nodded, a tiny bit of color returning to her olive cheeks. Stefano had raised hell to get Em back, leaving a bloody trail of bodies in his wake.

"Stefano was never present for any of those meetings," Nicole confirmed. "I wish I had more information for you. It wasn't for lack of trying, but I swear Antonio knew I would try to eavesdrop and had doubled the soldiers outside his office, so

I couldn't get within hearing distance. Your best bet is to talk to Frank."

"But you do think they were conferring about the Russians? What gave you that clue?" Emiliana's soft voice cut through the tension of the room.

"I do." Nicole nodded, her body stiff. "He'd cursed the worthless connection between Camila and Vic Pavlov and whatever favor Frank Rossi got from that union."

"Camila." I leaned forward, curious about Frank's daughter, Stefano's older sister. "We haven't heard a word about her since Frank shipped her to Russia. We didn't even know if she was alive." The Mafia wasn't the easiest place in which to exist. Alliances were necessary, but the cost could be too great. Frank Rossi was one of the bosses I didn't like. He was cold, cruel, and had sacrificed his daughters—Camila to the Bratva and Marissa, before she was killed, to Tony Caruso, Antonio's son—to gain whatever favor or power he'd craved. One daughter was dead, the other thought to be.

It looked like the Russians were behind both Marissa's death and the trafficking ring, even though we'd assumed Tony had killed her in a fit of jealous rage.

"Why is this coming up now?" Nicole asked, worry evident in her clenched fists and the tremor in her voice. "Does this have to do with Elena?"

Oh shit.

Tears misted in the older woman's eyes, making them as vibrant as new grass after a spring rain.

"In a way." Emiliana stood then seated herself next to Nicole, putting a comforting hand over hers. "Ivan is in town, and we're trying to figure out why and what part, if any, the Bratva played in our abductions four years ago."

"We don't know if Ivan is acting alone or if he's here on his father's orders," I added.

Nicole's head snapped back as if slapped. "Ivan was here

briefly before Christmas." Months before. "He spoke with Antonio."

Em met my gaze with murder in her eyes. "Do you remember anything at all about that time?"

"Elena wasn't home. Neither was Tony. I was grateful about that because that man reeked of evil." Nicole shivered, and Em squeezed her hand again, her fingers whitening briefly. "He didn't say a word to me, but the way he looked at me sent all kinds of warning bells off in my head. I got the hell away when Antonio led him into his office."

"That was it?" I had to be sure.

"He was only here for five or ten minutes. I watched from an upstairs window until he left. But whatever he was here for, it couldn't have been good." Her gaze bounced between Em and me. "Talk to Frank. Better yet, get Stefano to help get the information from him. It won't come easy or willingly."

Not long after that, we thanked Nicole then took our leave. As the miles dissolved between the Carusos' house to Em's, I couldn't help but wonder what the hell we would uncover and if it would cause a war to erupt between the Five Families—and possibly the Russians.

I dropped Em off and waited until after she'd walked through the doors to her house to leave. Hearing that Frank Rossi could have been involved with what had happened and with why Ivan had shown up had shredded both of us. It wasn't a confrontation Em would have. Instead, she would go to Stefano, his son, the one who had pulled her from that hellhole she'd been left in.

Before she got out of the car, we'd talked about who would bring it up to Stefano. I wanted to spare her additional pain, but she'd insisted it was her. I backed down because there was a bond between the two of them that I didn't want to mess with.

I put the car in drive when the front door shut behind Emiliana. My phone rang, and I squealed at the name that flashed across the console's screen. I hit the accept button so I could talk over Bluetooth to Lil.

"What are you doing calling me at this hour? It's got to be the middle of the night in Italy." I pulled through the circular drive and headed to the gates that led to the street.

Lil's warm, carefree laughter bridged the miles between us. I was truly happy for her and how she'd ended up with the love of her life.

"Yeah, well, I've heard things."

"What could you possibly have heard? You're on your honeymoon. You shouldn't be leaving the bedroom unless it's to rehydrate. You must be doing something wrong."

"Ha! Not even. And stop changing the subject." Lil lost the carefree tone, taking on that serious one I didn't want to hear. "Why is Ivan there?"

"That's what we're trying to figure out." I relayed what we'd learned from talking with Nicole. "I've got nothing else. Ivan hasn't been very forthcoming when we've chatted, other than to play his stupid mind games."

"What the hell did Eva see in him in college?" I could imagine Lil's eyes rolling.

"She's hormonal. I swear." There was no explaining Eva, other than how she, too, was in love with someone she couldn't have.

"I'll see if I can find anything out on this end."

"Thanks, Lil. I miss you but hope you're making tons of memories with that gorgeous husband of yours."

"Believe it." She laughed softly. "I know I told you, but I'm confirming that we'll be in Milan for your show."

Happiness warmed me. Their plans had been up in the air, and it hadn't been a sure thing, as Max was boss, and they weren't going to stay that long, originally. "I thought you were leaving for home a few days before the show."

"As if I'd miss being there for your first fashion show? Your designs kick ass. Besides, it's been a while since a Mafia princess has dominated the fashion industry, and there's bound to be some bloodshed. I wouldn't miss any of it for the world."

She was referencing Mom, who had been a model. A fight had broken out at one of her shows, and she had been on the catwalk, trapped as bullets flew by her head. Dad had claimed her from the runway, literally, and she'd never looked back.

I couldn't help the grin that spread across my face. "We'll make history."

CHAPTER SEVEN

SOFIA

After I hung up with Lil, the pain of lying about Elena to everyone I'd kept at bay crashed down on me like a tsunami. I couldn't go home. I felt restless and trapped. The memory of what Emiliana had been through, of how she'd looked when Stefano brought her back, played like a movie on repeat through my mind. Then there was my fear for Elena, the uncertainty, and a sense of loss. I worried for her but couldn't do or say anything to alert anyone else.

I lived a lie so she could have a life.

My body was shaky, agitated, and so very restless while my mind whipped from one thought to the next. I gasped for air as if I couldn't get enough to fill my lungs. The world was pressing in on me, and if I didn't do something, I would go crazy. In a last-minute decision, I made a sharp turn onto the highway. A contingent of cars squealed behind me as they adjusted to my maneuver.

I did not doubt that my brother would be informed that I'd deviated from returning home—possibly Enzo too. I got that what I was doing wasn't smart or safe. I did. But I needed to think, and even the thought of going home made me feel stifled.

It was bad enough that I had an entourage of guards following me. So I let the car fly, the power beneath me seeping into my starving bones. The illusion of freedom calmed my panic attack even though I would never truly be free. But for a few seconds, the pain of things that had happened or could happen eased.

Getting lost in creation in my studio would have been ideal. But they wouldn't let me, not with Ivan on the loose. Working at home was fine, but sometimes, I wanted to be away. To pretend.

I wanted to feel the speed of the car a little more then at least swing by the studio because I'd left my favorite waist-length fake-fur coat there. That was the excuse I would give everyone —the secret would stay buried inside me. I was thankful for the drive along the highway. It helped me shove my uncertainty and worry back down where no one would see it.

Tom's sedan was on my ass as I pulled into the underground lot. I prepared to let them see the mask I wore to hide the fear, projecting instead the spoiled princess they were used to dealing with. I mentally shrugged. No one said I didn't make his life interesting. When I turned into a parking spot and shut the engine off, Tom had my door open and blocked me from getting out of the car with his big body.

"What're you doing, Princess?" Tom growled, his green eyes boring into mine.

He'd been my family's captain for years, and we joked together from time to time. "Princess" was a term of irritated endearment that I'd rightfully earned. One thing he liked to do was assign guards to me who had pissed him off in some way because he knew that I would keep them on their toes with my quick deviations from my prescribed schedule.

I understood why Tom was annoyed with my unscheduled stop at the studio. Going in dark—into an area they hadn't secured—wasn't ideal, and I knew that. "What did you expect?" I blinked at him, assuming my most innocent face while fighting the urge to tug on the short hairs of his beard to see what he would do.

A mischievous glint sparked in his eyes.

"No." I reared back. "Who did you call?"

His lips twitched. "Marco." At my scowl, he added, "And Enzo."

Checkmate. I fixed him with my best glower. "This isn't over between us, Tom. You may have won this round, but wait until you're on Sofia duty next time."

"It's for your own good." His eyes flattened, and I rolled mine at his put-out attitude.

"Fine." I nudged his solid chest to get him to back up. He did, but not because I had any physical influence on him. "I take it you aren't going to let me go up there?"

He shook his head. "I'm sending Jim. What did you need so badly you couldn't have gone home and asked someone to retrieve for you later?"

I described what it was and where, frustrated that I couldn't even go up to get it myself. "Since we're here, I'm getting a coffee from across the street." I narrowed my eyes with my fiercest stare, the one that told him I would lose my mind if I didn't get my caffeine fix. He'd been on the receiving end of that before. It wasn't pretty.

Indecision warred across his features, but he gave me a slight nod. He must have anticipated it and sent guys over there. They had the best coffee, and he had to have known I would want to go once I'd parked.

I got out and locked the car behind me, surrounded by four guards. I was right. One went to get my coat, and the other three scoped out the coffee place to ensure it was safe. Marco or Enzo were on their way to yell at me if nothing else. I couldn't seem to get away from the testosterone overload. I was starting to think my slight detour wasn't worth it.

The intoxicating smell of coffee beans surrounded us as we

entered. Tom sent one of the guys to order my drink and ushered me to a table where they blocked me from the rest of the patrons' view.

An ear-piercing screech of tires, followed by the crunch of metal and shattering glass outside caused me to lurch to my feet as the guys around me pulled out their guns. Fear licked through my veins at the accident. *Please don't be my brother. Or Enzo.*

When I peered around Tom to see through the large window, I sagged against the table and released the breath I'd been holding. A green sedan had collided head-on with a white van. My pulse settled. It was horrible, but I was thankful it wasn't anyone from my family. The unease of feeling as if I had a target painted on my forehead had me on edge. I didn't want my family to be collateral damage.

I needed to slip away just for a moment to get control of my ping-ponging emotions. I tugged on Tom's arm and whispered that I was going to the bathroom.

"Wait."

I did as he requested. He spoke into his communication device to the guard at the rear entrance. Once he got the all clear, he nodded at me to go ahead. For that tiny bit of space, I was glad. Going to the bathroom and having the guards stand outside the door wasn't something I wanted to deal with. I was sure everything would be fine.

I was wrong.

My first clues should have been how dark the hallway was and that there was no guard there. There should have been. It was eerily quiet and devoid of employees, and there was no additional guard at the end of the hall, not that I could see well in that inky abyss. The last and most important clue was the scent of spearmint.

He came at me like a sudden storm. I never had a chance to draw my gun. Emiliana had known what she was doing with hers at her side when she'd left the house earlier. With the guard stationed at the back entrance, I hadn't thought I would be taken unaware.

All six foot three inches slammed into me. I knew it was Ivan even before he spoke. That smell of spearmint wrapped around me, raising all the fine hairs on my body. Ivan's hand was tight around my mouth as he pushed me into the one-person restroom. I tensed to fight, but a knife at my neck held me immobile.

The blade pierced my skin enough to draw a few drops of blood. My heart pounded against my rib cage, echoing in my ears. Light-blue eyes devoid of warmth bore into mine. I felt like a bug under a magnifying glass.

I would not die that way, in a public restroom at the hands of a Russian coward. My fingers inched behind my back, reaching for the gun I'd shoved into my waistband. The other was in my purse I'd left on the table. I was just glad I had the foresight to bring two.

A menacing sneer pulled at his lips, and I whipped out the gun and pointed it at him. Before I could squeeze the trigger, he slammed his free hand into my wrist, knocking it from my grasp. As the gun clattered to the floor, he yanked the blade from my neck. If he hadn't, I would have finished what he'd started as I stumbled forward from the impact of his hit.

I could sense my window of escape diminishing. Sweat beaded along my hairline. I would not give up. I blocked the pain in every attempt to find a means of overpowering him.

His large hand gripped my face in a punishing hold, and I wrapped mine around his wrist, digging my nails into the taut flesh. Time slowed as he raised the knife and ran his tongue along the blade, lapping up the traces of my blood. Bile surged. He was sick. Katya wasn't kidding. If I didn't find a way out, I would die a horrible death at his hands.

Pleasure lit within his twisted gaze a second before he

shoved me against the opposite wall. Dipping his head to my neck, he inhaled. On an exhale, he said, "Pretty little toy."

I bit down on my tongue to stop the whimper of fear. *No!* I slammed a lid on my emotions. I was better than that. My brothers and father had trained me well. I would not die easily.

I went pliant in his grip in an attempt to relax his hold, to make him think I wouldn't resist. I dropped my arms while maintaining eye contact with the biggest monster of them all.

My fingers curled around one of the hidden knives in my pants. I inched it free, intent on stabbing him multiple times until I severed as many major arteries as possible. The tight hold on my face would be the first to break. If I could surprise him and arc the knife to slice the flexor tendons in his forearm and wrist, he wouldn't be able to grab my face, let alone another weapon. It was a risk and an awkward cut, but Marco had trained me well. My free hand curled around the base of his hand, and I let all the fear that churned inside me show in my wide eyes, trying to keep him off guard.

The door flew open as I tightened my hold. I expected the calvary. Long blond hair swung into my peripheral vision. *Are they working together?* Another jolt of terror shot through me, but I ignored it.

"She's not yours." The barrel of a gun jammed against his temple.

Ivan shifted his head enough that I could see the cold fury in Katya's face. I inched my arm up, the small blade gripped tight between my fingers.

"Why are you here?" Ivan growled.

Katya's gaze never deviated from his face, but I knew she was aware of what I was about to do. "Your brother sent me." She lodged a knife into Ivan's shoulder, her hand moving so quickly, I almost didn't catch it. "Sloppy work killing the guard by the back door and leaving him in plain sight."

I jerked free as Katya's blade did what it meant to, and he

loosened his hold on me. She pulled me to her side, and I went willingly. A cauldron of fury and fear churned in my stomach, and I longed to cut him, but something bigger was at play, and I waited in silence, wanting to learn as much as I could. *Ivan's brother Vic sent her? Very interesting.*

Katya drew me behind her and out the door, leaving parting words for Ivan that left more questions than answers.

"Soon, he'll want me home," Katya warned Ivan. "Just remember, they'll figure it out. Then you'll be at the mercy of the Italians."

CHAPTER EIGHT

SOFIA

I cringed at Marco's bellow as soon as I stepped inside our house. Then I was wrapped in his strong embrace, the familiar spicy scent of his cologne adding another layer of comfort. "What the hell happened?"

I'd kept the terror at bay long enough. In his protective embrace, I let the tears fall. His arms tightened, and he waited until I was ready to speak. When he rested his chin against the top of my head, I sighed. The tears were already drying. Showing fear wasn't something I should have done, but it was Marco. If I couldn't turn to him, to my family, I would have been lost.

Several minutes passed where I kept my cheek pressed against his chest, letting him comfort me. We both needed it. I knew that the thought of losing me devastated him, and being able to physically hold me calmed his bloodlust for the Russians.

It was inevitable—I would have to confess as much as I could. Except Elena's secret, no matter how much Marco might have wanted me to share that one with him. It broke my heart that I couldn't. There had always been something between Elena and him, even though I thought I was the only one who suspected. I hoped that things would change, that she was well and safe, and that she could come back in the fold one day.

"I'm ready," I said quietly. And when he released me, I went with Marco into the study. Tom wasn't with us, but I knew Marco would talk with him next. He wanted time alone with me, and I was sure he hoped that would encourage me to tell him everything. Shame filled me for getting myself into that mess. I wouldn't have if I'd come straight home as he had demanded.

Dark colors warmed by the soft glow of Tiffany lamps on the end tables greeted us. Buttery brown leather couches and armchairs surrounded a coffee table. Marco led me to have a seat. Once we'd settled, his arm resting along the back, I tugged a pillow onto my lap and drew my legs under me, twisting my body toward his so we faced one another.

"What do you know?" I didn't want to repeat things if I didn't have to.

Midnight hair surrounded his strong face. Green eyes flashed with barely restrained fury. He had our mother's eyes and black hair but the angular contours of our father's face and his build. I had Mom's build but didn't get her height, while my eyes and hair were the exact shades of brown as Dad's.

"I'll tell you what I don't know," Marco growled. "What Ivan said to you in that bathroom for the handful of minutes you were in there, how in the hell a guard was killed, and how my soldiers didn't know until Ivan had you alone. And how did you escape?"

Great. So he didn't know anything about that encounter. I prepared for the storm because it was coming. In as few words as I could, I told him everything that had happened, even the part where Katya had intervened.

"Katya?" Marco was on his feet, pacing. He prowled back and forth, his fists clenching and unclenching. "Do you have any idea how deadly she is?"

"Yes, but I'm fine." I hugged the pillow tighter. *Where are my other brothers?* Usually, they would have been there, grilling me. Then Dad would too. Mom was the one who always saved me from the overabundance of testosterone, but she and Dad were on a much-needed vacation, leaving Marco in charge. It was one more indication of Dad stepping down as boss and swearing Marco in, which seemed like it would happen soon. Marco was more than ready.

"She's helped me twice now. You should be grateful for that. And I guess Ivan is acting outside of the family. Why else would his brother Vic send her to keep an eye on him?"

Marco stilled. "Because Vic wouldn't want a war, and that's what Ivan is attempting. What I don't understand is Katya's last statement. We need to figure out what she meant when she told Ivan that we would find out. I want a meeting with her."

The door slammed open, hitting the back wall and making me jump. Marco had his gun free and trained on our uninvited guest before I could take my next breath. "You almost got yourself killed," he snapped at Enzo.

Shit. I was worried about my brothers, but sometimes Enzo was a hundred times worse. I needed Mom to get me out of there more than ever. When she spoke, none of them would contradict her, and she would've pulled me out of the mess after I confessed what I already had because they would scold me repeatedly after asking the same questions in different ways. It was exhausting.

I got that they were afraid something could have happened to me, that I was almost lost to them. I understood where they were coming from, but I was upset and tired. That was why Mom would've gotten involved, had she been there.

Enzo ignored Marco as he stalked toward me, that muscle jumping on the side of his jaw. "You're not going to Italy."

I jumped to my feet, the pillow falling from my grasp. Any remnant of fear that I'd felt died a swift death at his words. He was in for a fight if he thought he could dictate what I could or couldn't do. "The hell I'm not!"

"Christ, Sofia!" Enzo's grip tightened, his fingers digging into my shoulders. "What were you doing with the Russian Angel of Death?"

"She's a friend." I hedged. The guilt was there underneath the resolve that what I'd done was right.

Enzo's dark eyes pierced my soul. "The last time she was here, she painted a room red with blood. She was found in the center of it, a smile on her face and knives clutched in her hands, still dripping with blood. She'd killed them all single-handedly. There were eleven of them." He gave me a shake. "She isn't a friend. Stay the fuck away from her."

I jutted my chin out and tried to jerk back.

The attempt was enough for Enzo to realize he'd held me too tightly, and he loosened his hold.

"I can handle myself. You're not my protector. Not anymore."

The monster that lived inside him rose to the surface, but I held my ground. He kept it in check most of the time with easy smiles and laughter. We all had such a monster, some more so than the rest.

The smile that curved his face caused me to suck in a breath. He was always beautiful, but when he smiled, even when it wasn't a nice one, it was impossible not to notice, and my mind went blank for a moment.

His finger hooked under my chin, and he tilted my face higher, his voice low, deep, lethal. "That's where you're wrong, Sof. I am. I always will be."

I couldn't stop my eyes from misting no matter how hard I tried. A chasm had formed, beginning when he'd told me about the arranged marriage between him and Elena. Sometimes, I wondered what he would think or do if he ever found out about my involvement with her. "No, Enz. That's where you're wrong.

You're not mine." My voice dropped to a whisper. "And I'm not yours either."

Enzo

The paper-thin line across her neck had me seeing red. I'd ignored Marco and pushed into the room, not stopping until I was toe to toe with Sofia. She tilted her head back to meet my gaze, her long mahogany hair tumbling over her shoulders and down her back. My fingers shook as I grazed the side of her neck, unable to tear my eyes away from the mark where Ivan's knife had been.

"We almost lost you, Sof. I can't risk it. If you go there, what's to say he won't follow? There will be so many people at the show. It's too easy to infiltrate."

Her amber eyes softened, and she curled her fingers around my wrist, pulling my hand down until she threaded hers with mine. Palm to palm, I sensed rather than felt the matching scars and the connection they signified.

"You'll be with me. No one will get to me," she whispered, soothing the beast that raged inside me. "Max will be there too. I spoke with Lil earlier. You can call in the Sicilians if Max hasn't already alerted them. We'll have an army, but I will not miss my first fashion show where my designs are featured."

"Leave now," Marco interjected. "It's doubtful Ivan will expect it since the plan wasn't to go for a couple of days. We won't tell anyone Sofia is gone. The rest of the luggage will come on the jet when Eva flies out. Just take enough for a couple of days."

It wasn't a bad idea.

"I'll call Max. He might have another off-grid house." Marco pulled his phone from his pocket and got to work on securing somewhere for us to stay.

I gave in and drew Sofia into my arms, cradling her head to my chest. "Sof, I can't survive something happening to you." I'd kept my distance from her, pushed her to arm's length in an attempt to keep her safe. *And look what happened.* She wasn't even around me, and she'd been targeted. I wasn't entirely convinced that what was going on wasn't about striking at the next generation of bosses. I would still be cautious, but I wasn't staying away from her any longer. I didn't know if I could remain emotionally distant, either, and I wasn't sure I wanted to.

I drew her farther from Marco so we could talk in private. My gaze traveled over the curve of her cheek, the pretty V in her upper lip, my thumb tracing over her full bottom one on its own accord, then back to her captivating eyes. I couldn't help but touch her, needing the assurance that she was warm, alive.

The pads of my fingers skimmed over her smooth cheek then buried into the thick mass of her silky hair at the nape of her neck. My gaze dropped to her mouth. When they parted, I almost lost it.

"It's all set," Marco said, breaking the spell she had over me. "Enzo, you need to go then meet her at the jet. I'll have several cars leaving to confuse Ivan if he's watching the house."

I tore my gaze from her lips, forcing myself to drop my hand, to step back and put distance between us. I felt the loss of her soft curves instantly.

If it hadn't been for her brother's interruption, I would have devoured her. On a good day, my control was shaky. When her life was threatened, I had next to nothing holding me back from needing her, making her mine.

"Go pack." Sofia jerked from my hold, guilt and confusion warring across her expressive features. I wanted to reassure her, and I would have if I could've gotten control of how I was feeling.

Marco waited until his sister left the room, a quiet click following her as she shut the door on her way out. I could count the seconds until the explosion. It was what I would have done if Emiliana had been in the same position.

"You hurt my sister, and I will gut you." Marco's green eyes narrowed to slits. "You wouldn't be going with her if it wasn't for the fact that I have to stay here and both of my brothers are unable to get away right now."

"I won't hurt her." The words left my mouth, but in my heart, I knew I probably would. A part of me had died when Emiliana and Elena had been taken. I didn't know if I was capable of giving Sofia what she needed.

Marco rubbed a hand over his face before he put his gun back in the holster strapped to his chest. "I understand why you haven't furthered what's always been between you and my sister." Naked pain tightened his features, his mask slipping before he regained control. "Em is back. She's strong—a survivor. When Elena didn't return..." He shook his head, the misery back full force.

I hadn't known he had feelings for Elena. I didn't think anyone had. "So you understand." Nothing more needed to be said. The hole that existed inside Marco was the same one that lived in me. It had damaged us to a point where I didn't think we could ever recover.

"I do. And I'm sure you get that I want better for my sister." He sighed then went to the door. "Be honest with her. I won't stand in the way of what she wants, even if she fights it as much as you do. All I can do is be there for her, make sure she doesn't fall. Don't be the one to push her to that point."

Incapable of speaking past the lump in my throat, I nodded. I'd heard what he had to say, and I would do my best to protect every part of Sofia, even if it were from me.

CHAPTER NINE

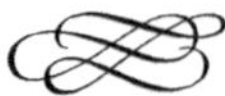

SOFIA

Night fell, and the rush from the house then to the private jet left my head spinning. I wrote a detailed list for my brothers and Eva of what to bring for the show. The only reason I wasn't putting my foot down and rejecting the new plan was that I had mostly everything that had to go at home after the mass exodus from my studio.

My heart hurt at how it was all going down, not at all like I'd imagined breaking into the design world for the first time. Ivan scared the hell out of me, and I hoped that Katya could keep him at bay. I had to believe she could, that we were moving off his radar, that he would be forced back to Russia. I did my best to push that worry to the back, preferring to concentrate on other things...

From beneath my lashes, I checked out Enzo, and my pulse kicked up another notch. We were alone on the jet and flying to an undisclosed location. All I knew was that he'd talked with Max and we had a secure place to stay that no one outside my family knew about.

A surge of annoyance swirled in my gut, and I lifted my chin to meet Enzo's smoldering brown eyes. Determined to get answers, I crossed my arms over my chest. "Where are we going?"

"Mondello. It's where Max and Liliana have been this past week."

"Will they still be there?" They'd gone to Italy on their honeymoon, and while I would have loved to spend time with my best friend, that wasn't it.

"No."

"I see." I ran my fingers along the condensation coating my drink. "Man of few words today. Got it."

His lips curved, and I let the silence lengthen. Everything had changed four years before, even prior to searching with Stefano for Emiliana when she was abducted. Not a day went by that I didn't long for what we had. I missed the stolen kisses. It hurt to look at him, especially when he wore that sexy crooked grin that caused my heart to speed or when he laughed and the dimple on his right cheek appeared.

I loved everything about him, even when he was angry. I couldn't resist all that muscle, the strength in his broad shoulders, the way he would move to shield me with his body. And when we touched, electricity followed in the wake of every innocent brush or caress.

But he wasn't for me, no matter how much I wished he was. He never had been, despite the way we had always been drawn to one another.

My finger absently traced the scar along my palm, a telltale sign that I was thinking about our past. He would recognize the motion and the sentiment behind it. I shifted my gaze to look out the window. It didn't matter if he did. Mentally, Enzo remained miles away from me at all times, just out of reach.

The minutes ticked by until he pulled out a laptop, and the fast click of the keyboard filled the silence. His family owned restaurants, the bank where the Five Families kept their money and where my brother Nico worked, and Envy, a very popular club. He could have been working on any number of things for the business.

Exhausted, I reclined my chair, determined to sleep for as many hours as I could. Putting on a brave face in front of my family took a lot out of me. The truth was that terror had simmered on a constant buzz through my mind and body ever since I'd locked gazes with Ivan across the street from my studio. He had said nothing, but the intent was clear. He was coming for me. I knew it. He knew it. And my family knew it, even if they didn't know why.

I didn't want to tell Enzo, given how bossy and distant he was being, but I was relieved he was with me. No matter what problems or secrets we had, he was my best friend and protector. It just didn't seem like it because for the past four years, we both had built walls that divided us. I was lucky to have Em and Lil, but I longed for Enzo in spite of what felt like insurmountable distance.

"Go in the back, Sof." Enzo's deep voice shivered over my body, and I opened my eyes. "You know there's a bed back there. No sense in sleeping in a chair if you're tired."

The problem was, I didn't want to be alone. "I will if you come with me. You can work there too." I didn't mean to show it, but the vulnerability I was feeling was probably clear on my face and in the soft plea of my voice.

His gaze bounced over my features before he gave me a nod. Relief swept through me as I got to my feet then headed toward the rear of the jet. I went into the bathroom with the bag that had my toiletries. By the time I'd finished brushing my teeth and washing my face, Enzo was stretched out with the laptop on his legs and the headboard supporting his back.

I went around to the empty side, toed off my heels, then climbed under the covers, fully dressed—no need to add more stress to the situation. I shut my eyes and lay there, hoping that sleep would come soon. It didn't. My heart ached, and I was overly aware of him next to me. I rolled to my other side, tugging the pillow into a better support position for my neck.

Light tapping on the keyboard cut through the silence, and I pointed and flexed my feet, thoroughly restless. Another flip. More typing. Then I heard the soft click of his laptop closing, and he set it to the side. *Is he going to leave?* My eyes popped open, and I angled my head so I could see him.

Knowing eyes met mine, and heat stained my cheeks at the way his lips twitched as if trying to suppress a smirk.

"Can't sleep?" His deep voice sent a shiver traveling over me, and my fingers tightened on the blanket.

"No." I didn't say more, especially not given what I was really thinking. Physically, he was close. Emotionally, we were so very far apart.

He scooted down then lifted his arm, beckoning me to his side. I went. The tears I refused to let fall added pressure behind my eyes, and I released the pent-up emotions vocally instead. "I miss this." What I wanted to say was that I missed him.

He wrapped his arms around me so that I was pressed to his side, his fingers playing with the strands of my hair. The only thing between us was the blanket and the wall that Enzo never dared to let fall.

"I do too, Sof," he whispered.

My greedy ears had to strain to pick it up. "Then why do you push me away? We were always friends, and for a while, more. Now, you rarely talk to me. We don't hang out together anymore."

"I miss those things too. I wasn't prepared for what happened to my sister. Want to know the messed-up thing about all of it?"

I squeezed my arm tightly around his chest. He was finally talking to me, and I'd listen to anything he had to say. "Yes."

"Seeing Em like that. What they'd done to her. It was a nightmare that I'll never forget. But the fucked-up thing was I couldn't help but think, what if that had been Sofia?"

Alarm spiked through me from the guilt and pain I heard, and I tensed. "But it wasn't."

"It doesn't matter. I can't unthink it. And if it had been you, there would be nothing to stop me from killing."

I didn't quite understand where he was going. "If you were so worried about me, then why did you push me away after you got back? It's been four years of distance."

"I have an irrational fear that if I keep you close, something terrible will happen to you."

"Enzo, there are always risks because of who we are, the blood running through our veins, and the families we're born into. That doesn't increase because we're together. And what happened to Em was a nightmare, but it wasn't your fault." Even the thought of what she had gone through caused bile to inch its way up my throat. And lately, with Ivan on my heels, it felt pretty dang close to happening to me too.

His fingers tugged a little too hard on my hair, and I ran my hand over his chest in soothing circles. Slowly, the tension eased, and the strain on my roots did as well. When he put his large hand flat on my back and added a little pressure, I complied, snuggling closer and tangling my legs with his as I'd done many times in the past, before he'd drawn back.

"I'm tired of pushing you away. I miss what we had."

"I do too." There was more I wanted to say, such as the fact that none of my feelings had diminished and that I loved him with my whole heart. It didn't matter. We couldn't break the marriage contract between him and Elena because of how we felt about one another.

And then there was Elena. She wasn't dead like Enzo thought. *How angry will he be when he finds out that secret?* I'd sworn I wouldn't tell anyone, but I wasn't sure that was the best course of action with Ivan on my trail. I would need Enzo's help to stay safe. If he didn't know why Ivan was truly after me, that could cause more of a rift between us, a chance I didn't want to take now that we were finally talking.

"We have a couple of days before we have to reenter the world." He smoothed my hair behind an ear. "Let's get back to us."

I didn't dare hope that he meant anything more than rekindling the close friendship we'd had while growing up with the other Five Families kids and my brothers around. My three brothers were always stealing his attention, and their friendship inevitably brought him to our house. He would spar with my brothers in the gym. If I wasn't at Em's house, I was in there, too, forced to learn to fight right along with Trey, the youngest of my brothers but older than me.

Other times, he would seek me out. We would watch a movie, play a video game, or hang out. That was the only time I was thankful for my brothers' influence when I was younger—they'd dragged me into the gym with them, so it didn't look like I was a stalker when Enzo was over, and they'd made me play hours of video games, which came in handy with him as well.

"What are you thinking about?" His voice was low and soft, delicious to listen to.

"Fighting and video games. Just about the times we'd spent together growing up."

He laughed, the rumble traveling up his chest beneath my hand. "Remember that time Marco made you spar with us but you refused to change from that sundress?"

I groaned. "Yeah. I told him there was no reason for me to change because I would probably be wearing something like that when I needed to kick someone's ass and I'd better learn to fight in it."

"I almost died watching you. That skirt flipped up so many times. Then when the strap broke and you beat the crap out of your brother for messing up your clothes." He was full-on laughing.

I pinched him, and he only laughed harder. "I'm still mad about that. I loved that dress."

"It was a damn good thing you were wearing those boy shorts instead of anything… smaller." A huskiness entered his voice.

I rolled my eyes, even though he couldn't see it. Even if I'd wanted to wear sexy panties, something was always happening in our house, and my brothers would have had a raging fit if we were sparring or running around and they had to see me in those. It was better to give in to some things. "Three brothers." I didn't need to say more.

"I thought I saw you at your most vicious that day."

"That should've taught you never to mess with my clothes." I laughed, knowing where he was going. Mom'd had my back that day. Clothes were her jam too. I wasn't the only one angry.

"Yeah, I finally caught on to that little truth. When Trey and Nico snuck in your bedroom and messed with your closet, I had no idea why that was 'getting back at you' for the time you threw their video games outside."

"That was no big deal. They could have just gone out there and gotten them instead of destroying my closet."

"It was raining."

I shrugged. "Eh."

His shoulders shook.

"They should have known what they were getting themselves into." I was pissed all over again just thinking about it. "I had to spend hours undoing the mess they made."

"You chased them around the house with a knife… for dumping your clothes on the floor." Between laughter, he barely got out the rest. "You were screaming at the top of your lungs. I'd never seen your brothers so scared. They thought it would make you mad, not crazy."

I smacked him on the chest. "Mom was pissed too."

"About you coming after them with a knife."

"Uh, nope. She wasn't upset about that, just made me exchange it for something else." I huffed. "She made them help me. You got to leave, but they had to spend the afternoon with me, hanging everything back up in the proper order."

When he calmed, I tapped his chest with my finger. "You're just lucky I forgave you. It was my stupid brothers who led you to the dark side. And despite what they probably told you, there are no cookies there. Knives. That's what's at the end of that path."

"I've missed this more than I could ever say." He squeezed me close to him.

The warmth from his body filtered into mine, and I relaxed further. "Then stop pushing me away." The words were out before I could filter them.

"I'm done with that. I'm tired of living in a world where I can't talk to you regularly. Where everything is black and gray. I need your vibrancy back in my life to breathe. I was wrong. I think I just needed time to deal with everything."

I didn't respond. I couldn't. My throat was tight with emotion, and my eyes were misting from gathering tears. What he was talking about was friendship. It had to be. And I would take anything I could get from him, even though I couldn't have him in the way I wanted.

He shut the light off from the switch near his side of the bed. "Let's get some sleep."

I snuggled in his arms, using his shoulder as a pillow. For the first time in a long time, I was where I'd always wanted to be.

CHAPTER TEN

SOFIA

My eyes were heavy, and the heat and comfort of Enzo's body made it easy to relax. Sleep wasn't far away. With the amount of time we had on the jet until we arrived at our destination, I preferred to pass a few of those hours oblivious and cooped up in the airplane's small space together.

The distance between us and all we'd lost only brought sadness. Those thoughts tumbled around in my head, making it easy for the past to slip through the lockbox in my mind and enter my dreamworld.

Katya was younger than I thought she would be. I don't know why that mattered. Stefano killed for the first time at twelve. The rest of the guys weren't far off in age either.

It was the blond hair and cold blue eyes that had my fingers curling around my gun, lifting it, only to have her knock it away. My heart slammed against my chest. "What do you want?"

Sadness swam in her light eyes. I wasn't buying it. This woman, the Russian Angel of Death, Katya, didn't have emotions. If she was there, that meant she had been sent to end my life, even if I couldn't figure out why. The odd thing was, she hadn't done it yet. That, too, was unlike the stories I'd heard. She struck fast, hard, and with finality.

"I don't want anything. I came to offer condolences."

Alarm spiked, sending another surge of adrenaline through me. "For whom?" Please don't let Emiliana be dead. We were to leave for college in two weeks, but she'd gone missing. No one had any leads. Stefano and Enzo had been gone ever since, hunting for signs of where she was, refusing to believe anything other than they would find her alive. Liliana and I had wanted to come to help. No one would let us.

"That she was taken." Her voice was low, sensual, and caused a shiver to travel through me. "There's another in your family that will be next unless you do something."

"Liliana?" Panic jerked me forward.

"Elena." Katya didn't flinch.

"What? How do you know? When?" I half turned, needing to do something, anything, to protect my friends and family.

"I hear things." Her thin shoulder lifted in a shrug. "And this type of suffering isn't something I'm okay with. I came to warn you. To offer aid."

How can I trust her? Her moral compass was off, yet so were all of ours in the Mafia. It was to be expected with what we did and because of the blood flowing through our veins.

My stomach churned, and bile climbed up my throat. I could guess what she meant. Is that what Emiliana was trying to survive? "My family will keep her safe." We were Mafia. It was what we did. That and retaliate. It was time we did that too.

"Not this time." Her eyes shifted to the right then back to me, and I felt the intensity all over again in the tightness of my skin. "We do this now or not at all."

"How do I know this isn't a setup?"

"You will be sending her away to an unknown destination. One only you and Elena will have knowledge about."

"Okay." There was no other option for me. If Katya wanted us dead, there would be no elaborate plan. She would do it before we even *knew she was upon us. I would help Elena, even though I knew I would owe Katya a favor one day. I just hoped I would survive whatever payment she would call due.*

Something pulled me from the dream, the memory, and my eyes flew open, frantically taking in my surroundings—*still on the jet*. I released a slow breath then took stock of my next problem. *Enzo.* Heat blanketed my back, and a heavy weight held me in place.

With the past so close, I didn't move. The memories needed to recede, and my heartbeat had to settle. The last thing I wanted was to explain to him what had me so uneasy. If he knew, I wasn't sure he would let me go to my show, and that was the only thing keeping me sane.

The steady rise and fall of his chest against my back soothed the unease that remained from when I awoke. I needed to focus on him, not on what I'd done or how I'd changed two lives with my actions.

There was a reason I hadn't fought Enzo putting distance between us. I'd had a hand in all of it. I didn't pursue him and force him to talk to help him heal. I should have. But I couldn't. The familiar guilt ate at my consciousness. I had to find a way to make things right, to get us back to the easy friendship we'd had. Luckily, we had time together in Italy for me to sort it out. After all, it was time we broke down some of the walls we'd erected between us.

He shifted, nuzzling my neck and pressing his body closer to mine, making me very aware of the fact that it was morning. *What would he do if I pushed back against his hard length?* My back arched a tiny bit before I stopped myself.

I needed to end it with him, no matter how much I didn't want to. There was too much left unsaid—too many secrets— between us for these kinds of games. I wrapped my fingers around his wrist to ease the weight of his arm off me. But he locked it down tight, pulling me even closer and burying his face in my hair.

My heart sped as he inhaled, and I almost moaned aloud. He was so sexy. I wanted nothing more than to indulge in whatever was happening, but he would pull away, as always, when he was more awake.

Better to end it than get hurt by his rejection. "Enzo."

"Mm-hm."

Killing me. His voice was deep and rumbly from sleep. I wanted to turn in his arms and brush my lips against his until he took control, deepening the kiss. Or at least that was how it went in my fantasy.

"You're crushing me." *Lies.* But if I stayed, there was a one hundred percent chance I would act on the moment, and that wasn't what he wanted. No need to make things more awkward between us.

Another second passed before he lifted his arm and rolled onto his back. Pain pierced my heart at what I was doing. It was a missed opportunity, one I didn't think I would get back. Shoving the covers off, I went to the window to pull the shade up. A ping from my phone made me pause, and I snatched it from inside my purse.

Before checking the screen, I glanced over my shoulder. Enzo lay there, hands clasped behind his head, eyes open, staring at the ceiling. Judging by the lost expression on his face, he felt the same as I did.

I released a slow breath, unsure what to do about our situation. Part of me wanted to say screw it and try to fix our relationship, even if I shouldn't take things to the inevitable point where they would go.

The rustling noise behind me told me Enzo was out of bed and getting ready. The captain spoke into the speaker, letting us know we would be landing in a few minutes.

Resigned, I dropped my gaze to my phone. *No.* My hand shot

out, and I pressed my palm against the wall. The text was from Katya: *I'm called back. He knows you left for Italy—not sure how—and that you helped Elena. Watch your back.*

I couldn't have helped the audible gasp from escaping if I'd tried. Ivan was hunting me, closing in, and I wasn't sure if I would be able to escape the plans he had for me.

Through the panic, I felt Enzo. Heat flanked my back just before his hands curled around my shoulders. "What's wrong?"

I shook my head. No matter how much I wanted to confide in him, those damn walls were still in place. Dropping my chin to my chest, I closed my eyes and told him what I could, all I was capable of sharing at this moment. "Remember when Alfonso was killed? We had made a pact, you and me against the world. That stopped the summer before I started college. You left me, and now it's *only me* against the world."

I stepped forward, and his hands fell away. Without a word, we exited the back bedroom and reclaimed our seats. Not long after, the wheels touched down on the runway. After saying goodbye to the staff, we got off the jet and into a car that would take us to the unknown villa in Mondello that Max and Liliana had generously loaned us.

Enzo dropped our bags in the back of the Maserati then opened my door, and after I was seated in the passenger seat, he got behind the wheel. Neither of us said anything. I needed to confide in him soon if I wanted a fighting chance against Ivan. My finger traced over the scar on my palm, and I took strength from our long-ago blood oath—one that was meant to bind us together no matter what obstacles we faced, a vow that would flare back to life once the secrets were gone.

CHAPTER ELEVEN

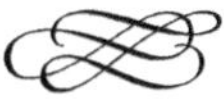

SOFIA

Enzo drove at breakneck speed, and an uncomfortable sensation traveled over me. I was too close to him in another confined space. His foot weighed the pedal to the floor. I was familiar with the demons that chased him. I had a few as well.

I pushed my sunglasses up the bridge of my nose, wanting to hide my conflicting emotions. The purr of the engine and the breathtaking sight outside my window helped me relax somewhat, and my mind wandered back to when I'd coaxed Elena to meet me not far from her house. We'd gone for a run, something she regularly did. I could still see her caramel-colored hair swinging behind her in a high ponytail as she jogged toward me.

Everything around me faded until I was fully in a memory of the summer before starting college. It was warm out, and the sun shone overhead. I had on yoga pants and a running top, but I would rather have been hanging poolside. But that didn't matter. I had a job to do.

Her security detail dropped back when I joined her. My feet slapped against the pavement, and I knew I would have to make the discussion quick because I wasn't in marathon shape like she was. Running was something I did when I had to—typically away from someone, usually from my brothers forcing me to build my endurance, not for enjoyment.

"Elena, slow down," I growled, my breath already coming too fast for the discussion we needed to have.

She laughed then did as I asked. "What's going on? This isn't normal." She motioned between us. "You joining me on a run."

I kept my voice even, hushed enough so only she could hear me as we passed the mansions in the gated community. We were heading toward the trail that meandered along a stream a few blocks away. "Katya sent me."

"What?" Panic forced her eyes wide. "Why?"

"She warned me that you're in danger, just like Emiliana. We don't have a lot of time."

She stumbled but quickly recovered before falling. Tension spiked the air as I waited a few seconds to continue until she had regained control. "Go home and grab what can fit in a purse, nothing that will be noticed. Then meet me at the edge of the forest where we had that party last summer."

"By the gardener's shack?" Her voice trembled.

"Yeah. And lose the security detail."

Our feet continued to pound the pavement, and Elena didn't look my way as she said the next thing, breaking my heart at what I was helping to do. "I won't be coming back, will I?"

"No."

"I'll be there in an hour." She kicked up the pace to a sprint, and I fell back, her guards racing past me.

I'd managed to lose my security detail. It would have taken a miracle to do it twice in one day, but that was what had to happen. I turned on my heel and set off at a slow jog to where I had parked my car. I had everything I needed. There was no reason to go home, which would let me maintain the freedom I'd managed from my guards. Decision made, I took off to wait for her in the woods where Katya would meet us.

Once in my car, I drove the short distance to the forest preserve and parked in a secluded lot farther from the main one where most of the hikers had left their vehicles. I got out of my car, popped my trunk, then grabbed the clothes I'd made and quickly altered for Elena. They were unmarked and unoriginal, but they would help her to blend.

At the bottom of the bag, I had stacks of unmarked bills. It would be too risky if she made a withdrawal, and since my shopping excursions were legendary, no one would bat an eyelash if I took loads of money out, even if I usually used a credit card. I only hoped Nico, my older brother who worked at the bank, wouldn't question me.

The humidity increased once I was in the woods, and I was grossed out as I swatted a few bugs away. I was not an outdoorsy person. Give me a high-end mall, and I was in heaven.

After trekking along the trail that led to the gardener's hut, I settled on one of the large boulders to wait while flipping through my phone. There were a few articles I needed to catch up on in the fashion world. That was the perfect time to do it.

I was halfway through the third article when all the hairs on my body stood at attention. My hand curled around my gun, and I looked down the length of my arm, my 9mm pointing the way as I scanned the forest around me.

"It's me." Katya's slight accent clung to her softly spoken words.

"That's super creepy." I turned and glared at her. "Make some noise next time, and don't come up behind me."

She chuckled as she moved to stand in front of me. "How did it go with Elena?"

I shrugged then rested my gun against my leg and near my purse. "As well as can be expected."

"You're doing the right thing." She leaned against one of the other boulders.

Tremors traveled through me and settled in my hands. I clasped them tightly, fighting intense fear about Emiliana. We didn't know where she was. Her brother and Stefano had been dispatched to find her after learning she was missing three days before.

I was terrified for my friend. Enzo was beside himself about whatever his sister was enduring. And the cold fury vibrating off of Stefano had me stepping back when he and Enzo left the day before to follow a possible lead, one I hoped was wrong only because of what it was—human trafficking.

"You're thinking about what happened to your friend?" Katya pulled me from my dark thoughts.

"Yes." There wasn't much more I could say. Breaking down wasn't an option. I narrowed my gaze, picking apart her body language and noting a slight flicker of a reaction in those light eyes of hers. Katya knew something. "Where is she? What do you know?"

Sadness darkened her eyes. "Italy."

Where the guys are headed. "You're the one who gave a tip to Stefano?" I didn't even need to ask. Somehow, I knew.

"To the Rossi underboss, yes."

I sucked in a breath. "Why him? Why not Enzo?"

"I've met Stefano before. My path has not crossed with Enzo's."

A twig snapped, and we both whirled in the direction of the sound. Katya had a knife pinched between her fingers, her arm back, ready to release it. I raised my gun, my finger hovering over the trigger.

Elena's unique mahogany-and-caramel hair peeked through the foliage—she would need to dye it, and soon. I relaxed my arm, lowering my Glock to my side, barrel pointed at the ground. "It's Elena."

As Elena broke through the last line of bushes, shoving a branch from her face, air whooshed from my lips, and Katya lowered her weapon. When Elena noticed Katya, her eyes widened, and she immediately looked at me. "What's happening?"

"Exactly what you think," Katya murmured. "I was sent to warn you. Sofia will get you out."

I tilted my head. Something was weird about their exchange. I felt like they spoke in code, but they didn't. I waited, listening to what they would say next, hoping for more clues.

"For how long?" Tears misted in Elena's eyes, but she didn't let them fall. Her spine snapped straight, and she shoved her shoulders back.

Blond hair shimmered as Katya shook her head. "I don't know. Assume there is no end."

Elena's clipped nod was all I needed. I grabbed my oversized purse and pulled out the pants I'd designed with several hidden weapons sewn into the seams and secret pockets, a dark gray shirt, and a nondescript hoodie. "Change into these. You can't be seen in those clothes."

She stripped out of her jeans, fitted T-shirt, and designer jean jacket, leaving them in a pile before pulling on the clothes I handed her. I showed her where all the weapons were while Katya took her old clothes.

Katya dropped the items in the dirt before picking them up. "I need your DNA on these."

"Why?" I swung my head to Katya, but she eased between Elena and me, an IV needle and tube in hand.

"She needs to disappear, and the best way to do that is to find evidence that she could not have survived."

My gaze shot to Elena, but her resigned expression held me in place as Katya inserted the needle then applied the blood in strategic places on her shirt. The soft pink material soaked it up. She dripped the dark-red liquid from the small tube on the neckline, gut, and where a kidney would have been—fatal wounds. Then she added some to the inside of the jacket, treating it as if she'd worn it while stabbed.

A few drops hit her pants, soaking the waistband in a few places, even running along the back as if she'd crumpled on the ground and the blood took that path. It was frighteningly perceptive.

Once she removed the needle, capped it, then tossed into the same bag, the jeans and jacket followed. She used the knife to cut through the tee in the center of where the gut and kidney wound would have been. Then she shoved that, too, into the waiting backpack, along with a few strands of hair Katya yanked out of Elena's head.

Katya handed Elena an orange juice then stepped back, putting distance between us. "It's unfortunate we didn't meet under better circumstances." She tossed a burner phone that Elena caught. "Call me only if you think you've been found."

With a nod to me, Katya melted into the surrounding forest. We didn't hear a sound from her exit. Time was ticking, and I needed to get Elena out of there before something equally horrifying to what had happened to Emiliana happened to her.

The car lurched to a stop, and the past fell away as I once more became aware of our surroundings. Enzo turned the car off, and my mouth dropped open. We were in the driveway of a home set into the hill, overlooking the Adriatic Sea. "Where are we?"

"Mondello. Max and Lil's place."

Excitement stirred for the first time since we left Chicago, and I hoped with all my heart that nothing would go wrong to ruin that slice of paradise.

Enzo

The car hugged the road as we curved around the bend. Sofia's withdrawal concerned me as I pulled into Max's driveway. She snapped out of it to ask where we were, and a little life sparked into her expression as she took in the view.

I got our bags as she stepped out of the car, exhaustion clinging to both of us. It was close to lunch, and I hoped the kitchen was stocked. The constant growl in my stomach for the last few miles of our drive had grown louder. Sof must have heard it and looked over her shoulder, grinning at me.

I retrieved the keys that I'd gotten from Sal, a Caruso cousin and soon to be second-in-command when Max returned to Chicago, from my pocket.

The place was amazing from the outside. I expected nothing less when we went in. I wasn't disappointed. An oversized marble tile I'd seen in luxury hotel lobbies covered the floor. The ceiling soared above our head, and the interior was light and airy, making the most use of the tall windows and accordion-style sliding back doors that led to the back of the house, which overlooked the sea.

I dropped the bags near the couches in the open-concept kitchen-and-living area. A fireplace was at one end with a natural mantel and a TV mounted above that. I took everything in, willing myself to relax despite the memories that hammered at the back of my mind from my time in Italy four years before.

"Check this out!" Sofia called, yanking the doors to the back open.

I followed. An outdoor kitchen and TV were under an overhang on one side of the back patio. But what she was mesmerized by was the infinity pool that merged into the view of the sea. A hot tub was on one side, and a sun shelf with two lounge chairs sat directly in front of us.

A blinding smile lit her face, filling her amber eyes with pure joy. I'd missed that look and hadn't been on the receiving end of it in far too long. That was something that needed to change.

"I'm changing and hanging by the pool. Join me?" She didn't wait for an answer but swept past me instead.

I had to fight against leaning into her as she sped by in typical Sofia fashion, energy crackling in the air around her. My shoulders eased with the return of her carefree attitude. She was usually upbeat and so charismatic that people gravitated toward her, a source of concern for her brothers and me. That sense of light and happiness was a part of her I wanted to protect.

Sofia vanished into one of the bedrooms as my stomach growled again. Crossing to the kitchen, I opened the fridge and pulled out food to make a sandwich or five. Knowing Sofia would forget to eat, I made her one then grabbed a couple of waters. I devoured two sandwiches, shoving the last bite in my mouth as she came out wearing a deep-red bikini. I choked. Everything about her was feminine, toned, and soft in all the right places. My eyes watered, and I gulped my drink to try to dislodge the chunk of food.

She winked then sped by me. I died a thousand deaths watching that small scrap of material hugging her perfect ass, which had just enough bounce as she walked to drive me to my knees. I curled my hands into fists to keep from grabbing her then followed with my eyes until she was outside and twisting her long hair into a messy bun on top of her head.

Resigned, I changed into board shorts and joined her. The flare of desire on her face when I took the other lounge chair, depositing two beers and the plate with sandwiches on the small table between us, went a long way to appease my ego.

Waves rippled across the sea before us in a soothing rhythm. A slight breeze chased away any sense of overwhelming temperature under the bright sun. She picked up one of the sandwiches and took a bite.

I needed to keep my mind off what I wanted to do to her. We still had unresolved issues—or I did. "We never finished our conversation from last night."

Sofia turned to me, her hand acting as a shade from the sun. "What do you mean? We both agreed that we missed our friendship. I thought this was us getting back to it." She motioned between the two of us.

"Hanging out. Yes. But that's not all I want."

She put her sandwich down. "Hmm, is this the point in our friendship where I need to set some boundaries? Because I won't be your maid. My brothers tried that crap when we went on vacation once. Do you have any idea what I did to them?"

I couldn't stop the grin. When she wanted to, she was able to make their lives hell. They loved every minute of it but would never let on. I knew that because I'd been on the receiving end of her wrath more than once. It was an experience, but the sheer amount of life that radiated from her was addictive. And the things we did, the life we lived, was refreshing. I always wanted more of her.

"I brought you food and beer."

"So? Marco likes to butter me up before being his usual jackass self." She narrowed her eyes. "Do tell, Enzo. What is it that you want from me?"

"You. I want you, Sofia, in ways that go beyond friendship."

"I'm not sure that's the best idea." A small frown tugged the corners of her lips down. "You've only just realized that you miss my friendship and that you were the one to pull away for ridiculous reasons, thinking that being near you would put a larger target on my head. I mean, I'm around my dad and Marco, who will be boss very soon. What makes being around you so different? Nothing. We need baby steps here, and friendship is where it's at."

I lightly shoved her shoulder, and she fell off the chair and into the shallow water with a splash. When she scrambled to her feet, anger lighting like an ember in her eyes, I was already up and around to her side of the sun shelf. My fingers grasped her wrist, and I yanked her to me, wrapping my arm around her narrow waist as I fell back into the water past the shallow part.

We sank back into the cool water, and it closed over our heads. Sofia struggled against me, the slide of her body erotic, sensual. I kicked to the surface, keeping us plastered together until she wiggled away, and I let her go. When she tried to touch the bottom, her head went under. I grasped her waist and pulled her to me, her head once again above the waterline. Her legs automatically lifted and wrapped around me. The feel of her was one of the pieces that had been missing. I felt it settle back into place while she was in my embrace.

Her arms had looped around my neck, and I was excruciatingly aware of every inch of her body. I slid a hand from her waist to her ass, cupped it, and squeezed. I groaned at the feel of her, and when her lips parted on a gasp, I spread my other hand over her nape and drew her closer. My mouth came down on her in pure hunger. Four years of pent-up emotions, of sheer longing for what I'd pushed away out of misguided self-preservation, transferred into the way I kissed her, devouring her lips, reveling in the taste of her.

Her response was instantaneous. The passion between us was electric, combustible. Neither of us were prepared for the explosion.

I angled her head and deepened the kiss. She shifted her hips, creating friction that had me stumbling back against the pool's wall as I strained to push into her. A moan slipped from her throat, reverberating through me and unleashing any restraint I thought I had. *God, this woman.* I needed her more than air.

When she tore her lips from mine, I tried to follow. Only her finger over my mouth stopped me from losing the final strings of my threadbare control.

"What the hell was that, Enzo?" she whispered, her voice raspy.

Her dilated eyes were wide as her pulse hammered at the base of her neck. The things I wanted to do to her. But she was waiting for my answer and had been the one to stop me from taking her in the pool, which had been the trajectory.

"That, Sofia, was something that should have happened a long time ago." I took in the wary expression lurking beneath the stormy passion still darkening her eyes and heating her cheeks. "I'm done denying how I feel about you." I caressed the side of her face, running my thumb over her kiss-swollen bottom lip. "You need space to process? Fine, take an hour or two to think about it, but by the way you responded, matching me in every way, I know you're ready to take things further too. And this time, I won't push you away. I'll be there for you no matter what happens around us."

Tears glistened in her eyes, and her lip trembled. "This is going too fast. I can't—"

"Shh." I'd gone too fast, thinking she'd be right where I was. I hugged her tightly and waited until she could gain control of her emotions, cursing myself for every second I'd caused her pain. If she needed time, I would give her that. But we were made for one another. With the arranged marriage contract between Elena and me no longer in effect, nothing stood in my way.

I meant what I said. Sofia was mine, and I wouldn't let her slip from my grasp again.

CHAPTER TWELVE

SOFIA

Enzo and I got out of the pool not long after the kiss. Holy hell, I couldn't stop thinking about it and what he'd said. Having him act on the attraction that had existed between us since forever was a dream, one that I wanted more than anything. But the truth about Elena stood sentry between us. I would eventually have to share everything with him due to the escalating danger surrounding me and the direction in which he seemed newly determined to take our relationship.

I took a sip of my warm beer—*yuck*—as I relaxed back on the sun shelf while Enzo swam laps. The sun glistened off beading water that clung to his skin with each powerful stroke as he moved him through the pool at a fast pace. He needed to burn off some of the pent-up desire that sizzled between us. I got it. I totally cockblocked him, but I did need to process. He was Elena's, and I hoped for her return—sort of. What I didn't want was for the contract to be honored. I would lose him all over again.

Will she come back? Given how things were, it was unlikely. And she could have met someone else and gotten happily married.

Content with the direction of my thoughts, I relaxed and enjoyed the gorgeous view—which was Enzo, of course. Now and again, I would check out the seaside panorama as well.

Several times, I worried about the upcoming fashion show. I'd snuck and called Eva to ensure everything was in order and that she would check in with the models too. It helped to ease my mind a little.

Half an hour later, when he finally rose out of the water in a powerful burst of rippling muscles—I checked for drool 'cause *come on*—I'd made a decision. It had been years with no word from Elena, nothing about returning. I was basing his future and mine on something that might never happen. And I didn't want to waste any more years to what-ifs. I was going to take what I wanted all along. Enzo would be mine. Maybe not that night, because that was just crazy. We needed some time to settle as we'd reestablished our friendship mere hours ago, and I wasn't going to risk it.

Another reason I had to wait to explore whatever was between us when he'd kissed me were the memories I knew were tormenting him as soon as we stepped off the jet. His body was strung tight. And while sex would distract, it would only be a Band-Aid. There were ghosts he needed to exorcise, and it was my job as his friend to help him. I couldn't put my selfish needs above his mental health.

Lost in my head, I didn't notice him standing in front of me until the sun was blocked, and I shivered. In a slow perusal—I couldn't help it—I let my eyes wander from his toned thighs to a trim waist that widened into a stacked chest and broad shoulders. I was salivating to get on my knees and lick the drops of water that had the privilege of clinging to his olive skin. I wasn't even letting myself think about his lips or what his hands could do to me. *Gah!*

I wrapped my hand around my beer and chugged the remainder for liquid courage. Once I thought I had a handle on not jumping him, I met his gaze and pasted a serene smile on my face. "Feel better?"

The wicked grin and darkening of his eyes told me more than I wanted to know. I needed to defuse the heat that sizzled between us. It was damn near explosive.

"Have a seat. I want to know how you're doing being back here, the memories... are you managing okay?"

And that did it. My words were like a bucket of freezing water. His body went rigid, and the stricken look on his face made me want to cry. But we needed to deal with it.

"Enzo." I said his name softly, trying to lessen the verbal blow I'd dealt. "Sit with me. I want to know how you're doing."

He scrubbed his hands over this face then did as I asked. In a few long swallows, his beer was gone too. I had to get more. Spying the wine fridge in the outdoor bar, I got to my feet and padded over. I grabbed a Cabernet, opener, and two glasses from one of the cabinets. Totally convenient. I wanted a back-yard area just like that someday. For the time being, I was content to live with my family. Life was good for the most part.

Back at the chairs, I handed him the bottle and corkscrew then got comfortable again. Whoever had come up with sun shelves and loungers was a genius. I would have to let Trey know he wasn't all that smart. The pool inventor had him beat. Seriously, I loved the setup.

I heard the pop of the cork but was slightly distracted by the direction of my thoughts until I saw the bottle tip into the air, not at all at the angle needed to pour our drinks. "Hey!" I read-justed so I was on my side, glaring at him for all I was worth, doing my best not to ogle the way his throat worked or give in to the jealousy of his lips on the wine bottle and not on me. "That was for me too."

He lowered the bottle, and some of the anguish had dissi-pated from his expression. I crossed my arms over my chest, secretly pleased and willing to do whatever I could to help the process along. "Do I need to get my own Cabernet, or are you going to share?"

When he passed the wine to me, that same wolfish grin on his lips, I shook my head. I knew what he was hoping for, and I was not giving in to the fantasy. Placing my mouth on the bottle where his had been was a sure way for us to lose control. We had things to discuss. I was going to help him. Instead, I splashed some in my glass then set it on the table with an added glare. "If I wanted a Neanderthal to hang out with, I would have made Marco come with me. His manners are about the same as yours are presently."

He barked out a laugh, and inside, I purred because joy sparked his eyes once more. If I needed to alternate sass and seriousness to help him process what he should have a long time ago, I would.

"I know what you're doing, Sof." Enzo's mood shifted back to somber, and I matched it with a sad smile.

"I'll do whatever needs to be done to help you. It's time to talk about what you're still reliving. Being back here can't be easy, and I won't be a part of a makeshift splint when it would be better to deal with what's going on." I reached across the table and squeezed his forearm. "Talk to me. Please."

His head knocked back against the chair. Seconds passed before he broke the silence. "Italy used to be a haven until it wasn't. I can't unsee what we encountered those weeks. And no, I'm not going to tell you."

"Always protecting me." I laced our hands together.

He gripped my hip and lifted me to him and across the table. Once he'd settled me by his side, he passed me my glass, and then he fisted the neck of the wine bottle and took another long pull. "This isn't something I'll compromise on. I'll talk about how I'm processing, I guess, but not what I saw when I went into those compounds."

"I know enough." My hand rested on his chest, and I curled

into him, tangling our legs. "Emiliana talks to me. It helps her sometimes."

His body jerked, and the arm around my waist tightened painfully. I breathed through it, tracing circles on his abdomen. It wasn't long until he calmed enough for the bite of his fingers to ease from my hip. "I didn't know. I've tried to get her to open up, but it's been difficult, and I—"

"You don't need to worry about her not opening up to you. She's talking, and that's all that matters. It could be easier with me because I'm a girl and can listen without wanting to kill everyone in sight and fix everything for her."

His gaze met mine.

I snorted. "Don't even. I know how guys work. I live with an overabundance of them. And don't think I don't want to go on a killing spree from what I've heard, too, but that's not what she needs right now."

"I'm capable of listening."

I rolled my eyes so hard I would have listed to the side if he hadn't had such a hold on me.

He chuckled. "You almost fell." Then he bopped my nose with his index finger, the wine bottle a tad too close for my liking. "Feeling dizzy from that overdramatic eye roll?"

"Please. I'm a master at them." I was dizzy, but there was no way I would admit that. *Guys and their overinflated egos. Sheesh!* "Look, I know you're worried about Em, but I'll always be there for her if she needs to talk, and so will Lil. You know that. And if she opens up to us, that doesn't mean she doesn't need you."

"I know that. I want to do more for her, take it all away."

I hugged him with one arm. "But you can't. And if you don't fix you—that part that's raging inside—you'll end up hurting the ones closest to you."

He hooked a finger under my chin and lifted it until our gazes held. "I've already done that. I'm so sorry, Sof."

I shrugged. "You're here now and working on fixing what

you have control over. We'll make new memories here. Let the horrors of the past go."

"When did you get so smart?"

"I've always been smart. And if you want to inform my brothers that I'm more brilliant than they are, I wouldn't mind." I winked. I was joking. My brothers were awesome, but teasing them was one of my favorite pastimes.

"I love you, Sof. Always have."

I smiled because I got what he meant as a friend. There may have been a crazy attraction between us, but I wasn't going to overthink what he'd said. "I know, Enz. I love you too."

CHAPTER THIRTEEN

ENZO

I laced my fingers with Sofia's as we strolled along the private beach. She refused to strap a gun to her thigh because of the tan line it would leave but had a sheath with a small throwing knife held like a hair stick at the base of the messy bun on the top of her head. I had my 9mm in the back of my board shorts. It would have been foolish to go anywhere without a weapon.

Sand squished between my toes, and every once in a while, the waves would break hard enough against the shore to roll over our feet. We were almost off Max's beachfront property and to the neighbor's. We didn't need additional witnesses who could spread the word that we were there, so I guided Sofia to turn back. We were both lost in our thoughts, the silence thick but comfortable.

Two days of swimming, cooking, talking, and laughing together had passed. Every brush of her hand was like a brand. I gravitated toward her—I couldn't get enough. Another missing piece had settled in my heart from spending time with Sofia. I'd missed her, but I hadn't realized how much. I'd come to some conclusions over the past forty hours. I needed Sofia in my life more than air. I would do everything in my power to protect and deepen our relationship.

We had that day and night before heading to Milan and the inevitable chaos there. My gut churned at the thought of the danger she would be in. I was glad that Max would be with us along with a contingent of Sicilians. We would need an army to keep her safe from Ivan. I hoped it would be enough.

Sofia tugged on my hand, bringing me back to the present. "Let's go swimming."

I nodded. We were back at the midpoint of the beach, and our towels were on the two chairs we'd brought down. Tossing our weapons on them, we waded into the water. Frothy waves licked at our legs as we pushed through them to get to the sandbar. I kept hold of her hand. The undertow was strong despite the almost-cloudless sky. But underlying electricity was moving in as if a storm was coming. In the distance, a dark mass had accumulated. I guessed we had another two hours before it would be overhead.

"I love it here." Sofia flashed one of her brilliant, fun-loving smiles. "I was searching for homes for sale along the coast, and so far, there's nothing. I want a place here with outdoor areas like Lil and Max's."

"People don't leave here often. But I agree, this is a great place to buy." I tugged her closer, and her thigh brushed against mine. I bit back a groan at the contact.

"Really? You'd want to have a home here too?"

Only with her, but I didn't think she was ready to hear that. She had a misconception that we needed to work through my issues and bond again as friends. My nightmares weren't going anywhere. She'd already helped to ease them. And as for how close we were, I'd never left her mentally. But I'd struggled with being around her, given that I couldn't keep Emiliana and Elena safe. I had hurt Sofia, and that was something I would spend the rest of my life trying to make up for.

"I'll contact our lawyer and have him keep an ear out for anyone who is thinking of selling." My thumb rubbed back and forth against her hand, and I felt her shiver. Each touch between us sizzled with anticipation. I didn't know how much longer we could hold out.

"Have him look for me too."

"Will do." The water was getting deeper, and we paused because it would soon be over her head. I released her hand then wound my arm around her waist, pulling her to me. She rested her hands on my shoulders and wrapped her legs around me. Her eyes darkened, and her lips parted as my hands shifted from her waist to cup her perfect ass and squeezed it. "God, I love your ass."

A sexy little moan escaped her, and I lost all control. Her body slid against mine, and I lowered her to grind against her heat. One hand stayed on her ass while the other was on the back of her neck, holding her to me as I took her mouth in a hungry kiss. The first touch of her tongue made me growl and tug her impossibly closer. When she started moving her hips, increasing the friction, I dipped my hand between her legs and skimmed my finger along her clit.

I tore my lips from hers and kissed down her neck. Her fingernails dug into my shoulders as I nipped at her neck, making her cry out in pleasure. Christ, her responses were killing me. More than anything, I wanted to slip the small scrap of bathing suit aside and thrust into her, but that wasn't how I wanted our first time together to be. Sofia deserved better.

I would deliver on that later. For the time being, I wanted to make her come and see as much of her as I could. Her legs were tight around my hips, so I eased my arm back, holding her at a forty-five-degree angle. Her hands shifted from my shoulders to grip my forearms, the water helping to hold her so she wasn't straining to maintain the position.

I wanted to watch as she fell apart. My hand left where I

hovered over her clit and moved around her hip to settle back where she wanted me the most. The bathing suit was in the way. Hooking my finger, I pulled it to the side, baring her before me. So pink and wet. I wanted to feast on her, and I would later. That was only an appetizer.

With the pad of my thumb, I teased her sensitive nub. Her lower back arched, and that sexy moan danced over the sound of the water lapping at our bodies. I wanted to sink into her more than I wanted anything. Feasting on her as she writhed in front of me, I circled her clit then sank a finger into her heat. Her breath came out in little puffs. Moving in and out, I added another, stretching her then curling my fingers inside her. With another thrust and more friction to her clit, she fell apart. A scream ripped through her as she rocked her head back. Drawing her to me, I increased the rhythm then captured her mouth with mine.

Goddamn, she was gorgeous. I was never letting her go.

We spent another few hours at the beach, playing in the water and dozing in the sun. Both our stomachs were grumbling when we went back to the house. Sofia was in the shower while I put together a lasagna—there was already home-made sauce in the fridge, courtesy of Max's aunt Rosa. I salivated at the smell coming from the oven after it cooked for a few minutes. With only thirty minutes until it was ready, I went to get cleaned up, almost knocking Sofia over as she came out of the room.

"Oh wow." She inhaled, her eyes drifting shut. "That smells amazing."

"Yeah, my stomach is trying to eat itself. This'll be the longest half hour of the day."

She rolled her bottom lip with her teeth before releasing it. "So were the last few minutes. In the shower. Alone."

Then she brushed by me, her light and airy perfume lingering and driving me slowly insane. I had plans for her, but not until later that night. Her attitude amused me, and I grinned at her. We weren't in a hurry, and I planned to take my time. A handful of minutes would not have been enough.

I showered, shaved, dressed, then went back to the kitchen to find Sofia pale and shredding a card into the sink's disposal. A bouquet of red roses was haphazardly sticking out of the garbage.

"What the hell happened?" Alarm screamed through me, and I had my gun in my hand immediately. Not waiting for a response, I went to the front door, checking to see if anyone was outside. There wasn't a soul. I went to the rear of the house. The back doors were shut and locked. I hit the security button, and metal screens slid down the windows. It wouldn't stop someone from getting in, but it would give us a warning. Once that and the alarm was set, I rounded on Sofia. "Talk."

She backed up, her breathing not quite right. "Nothing. I—"

"Do not bullshit me." My voice was quiet, controlled, and I knew by the widening of her eyes, deadly. "If you don't tell me everything, we're all at a greater risk. Now, tell me who the flowers were from and what was on the card."

She slowly shook her head. "No one. I have no idea."

"You're lying." The oven beeped, and she jerked away from me. I let her go, and she opened the oven door then pulled out the lasagna.

Neither of us said anything as she got plates out, filled the wineglasses, and turned the oven off. I waited, letting her process for a few minutes. Whatever was on that card had scared her, and I needed to know what it was. After another few seconds, I couldn't stand it anymore. "It was Ivan, wasn't it?"

She whirled to face me, and I saw the answer in the storm in her amber eyes. "I don't want to leave. Please, Enz, not yet. One more night where it's just the two of us, and I'll tell you everything."

It was foolish for me to agree, but something told me his game was a long one. He would practice psychological warfare then move in for the kill. I knew it would be at the fashion show. That was why we had so many soldiers called in.

"That's not a smart idea, and you know it." I was vibrating with anger as she closed the distance between us. I opened my arms, wrapping her in my embrace. "I know it's from Ivan. We should get out of here since he has this address."

"He's long gone. And I don't want anything from him to come between us tonight. I swear I'll tell you what was on it and… the rest."

"There's more?" I couldn't keep the growl from my voice. "How long has this been going on?" A tremor ran through her body, and I hugged her tighter. She gently shoved my chest, I eased my hold, and she tilted her head back to look me in the eyes.

"There is a lot more, and things will make sense once I share them with you. You pushed me away for years. I'm asking for one night of space, of being happy and enjoying what's going on between us. In the morning, I'll come clean. There will be no more secrets."

It was a terrible idea, but I understood. I wanted the same thing. The place had become a haven for the two of us, and I didn't want anything to taint it either. Rather than saying anything, I released her and went over to the garbage, pulled the bag with the flowers out, then took it to the garage and tossed it into the bin. I couldn't stand having him in the room with us in any capacity. When I returned to the kitchen, Sofia was at the table with the candles lit and the lasagna dished out on our plates.

"Eight hours, Sof."

She nodded once, her solemn gaze boring into mine. I took a seat across from her and clinked my wineglass against hers. If that was what it took to topple the final wall between us, I would grant her the time and make it memorable.

CHAPTER FOURTEEN

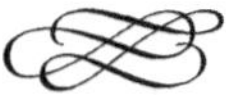

SOFIA

After Enzo and I cleaned up the kitchen, we went into the living room, where he started a fire. It was a minor miracle that he'd granted me a few hours. However, he had informed Max, and I couldn't even keep track of how many others, that Ivan was making a move in Italy and that he'd already initiated contact with his stupid psychological-warfare games.

Katya warned me not to take him lightly—he liked to break women. He needed to die. A tremor shook my hands, and I tucked them under me on the couch so Enzo wouldn't see. When he joined me with our refilled wineglasses, I took a few gulps.

"Want to talk about why you're so nervous?" His brows quirked up, and concern pulled his mouth into a straight line.

"Sure." *Not at all.* "We're taking our relationship from best friends to so much more. Of course, I'm nervous."

He tucked the hair that had fallen forward behind my ear, and I shivered in the wake of his touch. It wasn't enough—I'd wanted him most of my life, and the other part I needed was his friendship. Now, both were within grasp. The moment wasn't lost on me. It was everything.

"The past few years have been a lesson in survival for me. Without you in my life, the way we always were, I was barely existing. I'm done living that way. After one taste of you, I'll never get enough."

Shivers trailed over every inch of me at his words. Then he took my wine and set it on the coffee table. I was lost with the first touch of his hand. The world faded away. There weren't any problems waiting. There was only him.

I was helpless to resist the magnetic pull between us. He shifted, and his hands went to my hips, lifting me to his lap. Straddling him, I rested my palms on his wide shoulders, loving how the muscles flexed beneath my fingers. Any lingering nerves I had fled, and I closed the distance between us, brushing my lips against his in a soft caress. Before he could deepen the kiss, I trailed kisses from the corner of his mouth along his angular jaw and finally to his neck.

I could feel him lengthen and thicken beneath me, and I fought the urge to add friction by moving my hips. We had all night—there was no reason to hurry, and I wanted to explore him before he took control.

I ran my hands over his shoulders then buried my fingers in his thick, silky hair, giving the strands a gentle tug before moving to the hem of his shirt and lifting it until he took over its removal, yanking it over his head. Too many warring sensations swirled through my body as his hands bypassed my hips, where they had been, to span my ass, cupping and kneading. Heat built low, and I moaned, helpless when he rocked me into his hard length. The delicious friction teased me about what was to come.

I drew back from kissing his shoulder then swirling my tongue over his nipple when he whipped my tee over my head. My bra was next, and I shivered at the heat in his gaze. When his hands cupped my breasts, my back arched, and I gave in to his touch. A gasp escaped my lips as his warm mouth closed over my nipple while he caressed the other, rolling the stiff peak between his thumb and forefinger.

Eyes glazed with desire, I traced the tattoos that were inked across a portion of his well-defined chest, over a shoulder, and down part of his bicep. I'd always loved his tats, but mostly what they decorated. I'd wanted to get one on my hip bone but had refrained. Maybe someday.

"Sofia." His voice was thick with desire.

I nodded to the question swirling in his dark gaze. I wanted it too. There was no need to ask me. "I've always been yours, Enzo."

He grabbed my ass, lifting me with ease as if I weighed nothing when he stood. As my legs wrapped around his waist and my arms at his neck, I relished his strength and our skin-on-skin contact. *Heaven.*

When we were in the bedroom, his hands moved to my waist, and I let my legs slide down his body until my feet were on the floor. Fingers at the waistband of his jeans, I popped the button before he stilled my hands.

"I've waited for this moment for so long. Everything about you is so damn sexy, including that sarcastic mouth and brilliant mind. Let me love you, Sof, because you're all I've ever wanted, all I ever will."

I whimpered. There were no words. He dropped to his knees in front of me and peeled the rest of my clothes off. I trembled at the way he looked at me with both love and wonder.

"You're so beautiful." His large hands skimmed my thighs, dark promise swimming in his eyes.

Our clothes melted away, and my pulse fluttered at the base of my neck as he closed the distance between us, trailing kisses from my jawline down my neck. My fingers twitched with the need to explore the well-defined contours, and I traced his broad shoulders as they flexed, the skin taut under my touch. He crowded me until I felt the press of the mattress at the back of my thighs then lifted me with ease, lying me on the bed. He removed the rest of his clothes before following, and my hungry gaze tracked his every move.

With excruciating slowness, his hand moved up the outer side of my thigh as his lips captured mine, brushing back and forth until I moaned, and he deepened the kiss. I urged him closer, the heat of his body addictive as he angled my head, the need behind his caress increasing my own.

His muscles bunched and flexed as I explored his body, dizzy with want and desperate to all of him. He broke the kiss, and I moaned, quivering with need as his teeth scraped my neck. When his fingers dipped between my folds, I gasped at the burst of sensations that flooded through me, arching into him as he teased my clit then dipped his finger inside. My body hummed, hypersensitive to every touch. He increased the tempo, and I thrust my hips to meet him.

Passion between us built until I thought I couldn't take much more, my climax so close. "I need you now." I couldn't wait much longer. The hard press of him against my thigh tormented. His fingers played me, and his leashed strength rippled beneath my hands as I trailed them over his shoulders and back, urging him to enter me, needing the fullness only he could provide.

When he didn't do as I wanted, I wrapped my fingers around his thick length. He rested his forehead against mine, and his body stilled. A deep moan escaped his lips, vibrating against my skin. I pumped my hand in a slow caress.

He controlled my body, but I had power too. When he lifted his gaze to meet mine with predatory desire, heat exploded in my core, slicking the way for his entry. I arched my back, needing him to fill me, my legs shaking in anticipation.

His fingers traced my seam, and I cried out. Then his hard

length pressed against my entrance before he pushed inside and thrust deeply. I arced higher to meet him as feverish nerve impulses exploded at the contact. His lips took mine in a drugging kiss, making my head swim. It was too much yet not enough.

I clung to him, his corded muscles shifting beneath my hands with each powerful thrust. The passion between us built to impossible heights. Then he slipped his hand between us, his fingers dipping between my folds and teasing the sensitive bundle of nerves, and I exploded around him. He increased the pace. My body clenched around his in a tight vice as he chased my climax until he found his own.

We lay together, catching our breath. A deep laugh filled the room, and I marveled at the joy that sparked in his brown eyes, my heart warming at the sight. A few minutes passed until he shifted to his side, and I mourned the loss of him and how empty I felt as he withdrew. Then he rolled me so that he was on his back and I was tucked against his side, his shoulder a pillow for my head and his arm holding me tightly.

As the pounding of our pulses returned to a steady beat, my eyelids grew heavy. He traced circles along my arm, and I snuggled closer, my legs tangling with his. What we'd shared was more than I ever thought possible.

As sleep claimed me, the worry over how I was hurting Elena swirled in my mind. She'd suffered enough from having to go off-grid. Even if Enzo didn't take their marriage agreement seriously, I had to honor the fact that I didn't have a claim on him, even though I feared that losing him would break me.

I slowly stirred awake, blanketed by the heat from Enzo's body. My head rested on his chest, and his arm anchored me to him, our legs tangled together. I felt a delicious soreness from how often we'd made love last night. The first would be etched in my memory for all time. I'd never been worshipped like that before. Throughout the night, he'd reached for me, and we started all over again—*best night ever.*

In the wake of that thought came the crushing one about my promise. *I have to tell him everything.* And I meant everything. My arm shifted from resting against his chest to wrapping around his waist and holding on like he would disappear, because that was the thing—it was entirely possible he would, at least emotionally. I'd had him for a handful of hours throughout the night, but I could lose him for a lifetime. I couldn't bear the thought.

A quick glance at the glowing clock on the nightstand closest to him told me we had two hours before we needed to leave. It was dark in the room with the metal hurricane shutters blocking all the light, which is why we'd left the bathroom one on and the door cracked open. Neither of us wanted to be robbed of sight while we explored one another.

The ticking clock echoed loudly in my head. I needed to get up, shower, and get breakfast started if I could without waking him. Enzo was a light sleeper for the most part. We all were. From a young age, we'd been trained to recognize sounds that didn't belong and to wake ready to fight. It was survival.

In slow increments, I lifted my arm off his chest and untangled our legs. As soon as I inched away, his arm tightened around me, and he crushed me to him.

He flipped me onto my back, nuzzling my neck. "Where are you going?"

Sleep clung to his voice with a raspy depth that was incredibly sexy. A smile played around the corners of my mouth despite that I was attempting to flee, at least for a little while. I needed to get out of bed before it wasn't possible. Heat pooled low, and it was already becoming hard to think.

"Bathroom."

He lifted his head, brown eyes met mine, and I sighed. He was gorgeous. My fingers skimmed over his broad shoulders, tracing the ink on his arm. But it was who he was inside that meant the most to me. He made me laugh. In his presence, I felt protected, cherished, beautiful, loved, and unconditionally accepted.

"I know what you're doing." His words were soft as he rolled onto his side, his hand at my hip.

"I just need to go to the bathroom." But he knew me, and it was a stall tactic. There was no denying it. I don't even know why I tried.

"Go." He sighed. "Get ready. We'll eat breakfast before we talk."

A small nod was all I could manage. When he lifted his hand from my hip, I rolled out of bed and went into the bathroom.

"You're killing me," he said, and the comment followed me in there and lightened my mood considerably, although I didn't have anything to wear after I got out of the shower, having walked in there naked.

I only took half an hour to get ready. Wrapped in a towel, I went back into our room and grabbed clothes, got dressed, and hurried into the kitchen before he was out of bed. I heard the shower turn back on when I started the coffee.

The time went too fast. When Enzo came into the kitchen, I had breakfast dished up and coffee poured. We ate in silence. Then he pulled me to the couch, where we faced one another. I was out of time. He deserved to know. I hoped it didn't cost me him.

I fought the urge to lurch to my feet and pace. A slight tremor shook my hands, and I tucked them under my legs. "A few weeks before I left for college, Katya approached me."

His body tensed, and unleashed violence crackled in the air. I got it. He didn't like that she was anywhere near me and was barely holding himself in check. I had to keep going before he exploded and I got mad and refused to tell him everything.

"Emiliana was missing. Everyone was frantic. It happened after I got coffee and was walking back to my car."

"Where were your guards?" he growled.

"I slipped out without anyone knowing. I don't do that anymore. Well, I try not to. I only do it if I have to, like when I met with her the next time. But I'm getting ahead of myself. She pulled me into that small walkway between the coffee place and the building next to it. We had cover from the street, and holy shit, she disarmed me so fast. I got a hit in, and she laughed. It was… intense."

He ground his teeth, my cue to talk faster.

I took a deep breath and got to the heart of the matter, an avalanche of nerves taking flight in my stomach. "I was terrified for Emiliana, and Katya had information."

Stark pain flashed in his eyes, and a wince pulled at his lips. The only reason I saw it at all was because of how well I knew him. My hand rested on his thigh, the muscles rigid beneath my palm. There was a slight easing of his tension from the touch.

"I had to help, and Katya hinted at what was happening to Em. That it was a human trafficking operation that had her and also where she was being held."

A muscle ticked furiously along his jaw, and I dug my fingers into his leg to keep him grounded, focused on listening to me.

"Before you jump to any conclusions, Katya was the one who slipped the tip to you, Stefano, and Marco about where Em was."

"That she was in Italy or the name of the traffickers that took her?"

"Both." I let the word settle between us, a new gleam entering his eye. He wanted to know why. I got it. I did. Katya didn't do anything without a motive. "Anyway, she told me that she wasn't on board with what happened in those outfits."

"And you never questioned why she came to you?"

I pursed my lips, not liking the doubt he was throwing. There was a whole other part I was leaving out that I would get to soon. "Not at the time."

"What do you think now?"

"I know better. When Ivan showed an interest in me, I reached out to Katya. She confirmed what we'd all suspected. Ivan was after me—to find Elena."

"What?" Enzo leapt to his feet, his body vibrating with fury. "She died. Why is he coming after you, and why now?"

Tears flooded my eyes and spilled down my cheeks. That was the part I didn't want to share, where I knew I would lose him. "Because I helped hide her, and I know where she is."

CHAPTER FIFTEEN

ENZO

I shot to my feet and stood over Sofia as she fell apart. A part of me wanted to comfort her, while the other was furious. She'd lied to me. I raked my hand through my hair. *Why did she keep this from me?* Ivan would not stop his pursuit, which changed everything. The fact that Elena was alive was two sides of the same coin. I was relieved she hadn't died in the way we'd thought.

Then everything else clicked into place—why Sofia pushed me away, saying I wasn't hers. I looked back at Sofia. Her shoulders shook as she sobbed. The four years where we were distant was all me. I got that.

The knowledge she'd shared meant the arranged marriage contract between Elena and me was very much intact. Sofia's hesitation to commit to me made sense. It was something we would have to discuss.

Ivan knew where she was. He'd had flowers delivered the night before. I needed more people protecting her, and I couldn't take a chance on an ambush without backup. I should never have listened to her about how nothing more would happen, but I didn't regret that I had. "We need to go. Throw your stuff in a bag. I'm letting Max know we're on our way to Milan."

She swiped the wetness from her face with her fingers, jumped to her feet, and raced to the bedroom. I felt like a jackass for not consoling her. Later, I would make it up to her.

I palmed my phone against my ear, rapping the knuckles of my other hand against the wall. As soon as Max picked up, I unloaded.

"Ivan found us. We're coming in hot. Are you there?"

"How the hell did he find you in Mondello?" Max asked with a growl. "And are you both all right?"

"We're fine, but we can't stay. Not without backup."

"Right. I'll get everyone ready and together. You coming straight to the house here?"

The La Rosa family had a home in Milan because of Sofia's mom's modeling career. That was where we were going. "Yes. I'm not sure it's the best place to be, but since he found us here, our car must have been tagged. I'm leaving your place locked down with the hurricane shutters."

"Good. Stay safe."

I grunted then hung up with Max. An eerie feeling settled over me. Sofia was mine, and I would not let anything happen to her. The next call was to her father, Robert, who added Marco on the line too. After they were caught up, I hung up. Sofia entered the room, dropping both bags at my feet.

"I threw your stuff together too. Ready?"

She was pale, but the light makeup she'd put on helped to disguise the fact to the casual observer, but not me—never me. I would always see her. With her hair in a high ponytail, falling down her back in big curls, and large hoop earrings, she looked gorgeous. She always did, though.

Her eyes held me captive. Fear swam in the amber depths, which she masked by squaring her shoulders and with the gun at her side. She seemed determined when she pivoted, the bag's strap thrown over her shoulder. I bent and picked mine up, and we were off.

We didn't speak a word as we opened the door, and I scanned the way before standing directly in the exit. A gasp fell from her lips, and I jerked my gaze in the direction of her eyes. On the stoop, there was a spool of some kind of cord I'd seen her use for sewing, a card attached.

While she bent and scooped it up, my gaze swept the area. There was no one. The hillside road was quiet. The neighbors were too far away. Sofia plucked the card from the spool, and as she read it, her shaking worsened. I took it from her, shut the door behind us, then hurried her to the car. Once we were inside, the bags in the trunk, I let myself read it.

"The tools of our trade are intertwining. Here's a little something I look forward to experiencing with you."

"I'm going to enjoy killing him," I promised both of us. After clearing the gate, I pulled onto the street and sped as quickly as possible on the winding road. I did not doubt that we would encounter Ivan soon. It was a fucking game to him. The only part I was relieved about was that he was taking his time, which gave me more of it to find him, to draw him out so I could end him.

"I'm worried about how he found us," she said softly, but the gun resting on her thigh told me how upset she was.

"I'm not sure. I hope none of our soldiers were coerced to spy for him." I squeezed her arm then returned my hand to the wheel. There was too much at stake. "Your father knows. They're on their way after questioning every guard who was in the household or on the grounds the day we left."

"I can't even think of any of the soldiers turning. I've known most of them for half my life, if not all of it." Shifting in her seat, she angled toward me.

"I know. But we don't know if someone was desperate

enough or resentful, wanting to change an aspect of their lives. Ivan is… persuasive."

"Yeah." She shivered.

I regretted saying even that much. None of it was new to her, to us. It was just the way of our world. "We'll get through this, Sof. Try not to worry about who Ivan could have used. That part, we will figure out."

She nodded. Silence lengthened between us as I pushed the car to go faster, willing the miles to melt away to get us closer to backup. I didn't like being out in the open like that.

We traveled for miles before we had to stop for gas. After I filled the car, Sofia walked over to where there was an overlook, surrounded by foliage on one side and a large bounder on the other. We wouldn't stay long, but I felt she needed a small reprieve and a chance to catch our breath without rushing to what I had no doubt would be where Ivan would attack. He'd played his games at the villa. For some reason, it didn't seem like that was where the final showdown would be.

Sofia and I stood at the railing of the small lookout. The salty air caused her hair to curl and thicken even more. I pulled her to my chest and rested my chin on her head, needing to feel her against me.

"We haven't talked about Elena."

"There's not much to say, Sof. I'm happy to hear she's alive, and we'll need to decide what's best for her, but my concern is you. She isn't in immediate danger. You are. And if anyone tries to take you from me…" I couldn't finish the thought. My throat closed, and a wave of violence locked everything down tight in my body.

She turned in my arms and rested her palms flat against my chest then tilted her doe eyes to me. "Hey. I'm right here. Nothing is going to happen to me."

I cupped the side of her face. *How did I survive without her in my arms for the past few years?* She was always so tempting, and I was at constant internal war over what to do with her. That damn contract between Elena and me stole too much time. But it wasn't only that. I'd caused the rift after recovering my sister and because I'd failed to protect two women connected to me. So I'd pushed Sofia away.

No more. I was done. Nothing would keep us apart. Not the Russians or Elena. I had a plan for at least one of those problems.

I bent then brushed my lips across hers. "I love you, Sofia. Always have." Then I deepened the kiss, exploring the sweetness of her mouth. When she moaned, I had to fight not to take her against the railing.

When I broke the kiss, she clung to my shoulders, and an overwhelming sense of rightness filled me. I wanted her for the rest of my life. I pulled her close again, and she rested her head on my chest as our hearts returned to a more sedate pace. The waves crashed below, and my internal clock kept pace with how much time we had been there and not on the road. It was time to go. We drew apart, her hand sliding down my arm until our fingers threaded together.

Once in the car, I turned the engine over. With no idea as to when Ivan planned his next move, we were both aware that he could ambush us along the way. There were other Russians in Italy that could join him in the attack. I texted Max our location to have people ready to help us should we need it.

We tore out of the small overpass not far from the gas station and onto the street. It was early and not as crowded as it would be in another hour or two. Time passed without any sign of trouble. It wasn't until the hairs stood on the back of my neck that I knew our good fortune was running out. We merged onto the main road that would take us to the house, which was where I would have ambushed him had the tables been turned.

When three black cars pulled behind us, I knew who it was. "Let Max know they're here."

Sofia called him, relaying our location and how many were behind us as the first shots were fired. Increasing our speed, I swerved around cars. Tires squealed, then the black cars closed the distance. We went around a bend to the right, hugging the side. Sofia lowered her window, firing at them. Glass shattered, and we ducked. The rear window was gone. That made it easier.

Twisting my arm, I fired out the back, my gaze divided between the rearview mirror and the road in front. It wasn't going to work. We weren't losing them. There wasn't enough traffic to hinder their progress. I had to pull over and take them all out. "I'm stopping."

She lay across me, hitting the buttons to lower the rear windows. There was enough of a side road, and I whipped the car onto it, slamming on the breaks. Three cars maneuvered to the side not far from where we'd stopped. Both Sof and I got out, quickly opening the back doors to use as a shield.

Seven men in suits exited their vehicles. Russians. We traded bullets. Men were shouting, and a pop sounded as glass shattered. I wished that Sofia wasn't out there with me—hated it, in fact. Two men were down then three. We kept firing. When Sofia ran out of bullets, she rummaged under the seat and opened the compartment with more guns and magazines. Tossing two extras on my side, she released the empty magazine in her gun then slammed a new one home.

"Get inside. Shoot out the back." I didn't like her so exposed. She got to her knees on the passenger seat, shooting around the headrest through the rear window. Miraculously, they weren't firing at her—Ivan wanted her alive.

Four. Five. We almost got them all. Sofia lay on her side, firing from below the car door, aiming for their ankles. Two more fell. When they did, she put bullets in their foreheads. I laughed. Anger simmered in my veins, but doing that with her was fun.

I took out the last man. Neither of us lowered our guns.

There could have been more men in the last car. The windows were tinted. Only the driver's and rear doors were opened, not the one for the front passenger seat.

Then the door opened, and my blood ran cold. Ivan stood beside the car, laughing. I wanted to squeeze the trigger more than anything, but my hands were tied. Killing him would start an immediate war, and I'd been warned not to. I wasn't boss—not yet. I couldn't make that call.

"That was amusing." Sadistic laughter trailed Ivan's words. "I look forward to our next encounter."

He'd spoken to Sofia. It was unacceptable. I stalked over to him until we were inches apart, matched in height but not in ruthlessness. It wouldn't have taken much to bring out the monster that lived inside me, the one I hid with easy smiles and a laid-back demeanor. The psychosis he wore on his sleeve with his psychological games reflected in his light eyes.

Sofia was in my peripheral vision. So far, she'd stayed back. I would block her if she moved even an inch closer. Ivan would not touch her.

"Stay the fuck away from her, or I'll defy the order not to end you." I jammed my gun against his shoulder and squeezed the trigger. Ivan grunted. It was nonlethal. I couldn't kill him, but I wasn't ordered not to inflict a little pain. That would have been nothing to any one of us, but it did nothing to ease the murderous rage that flowed through me. "She's mine. If you go near her again, I'm acting on my own."

CHAPTER SIXTEEN

SOFIA

Four cars raced toward us, screeching to a halt around where we'd parked. My heart pounded, and I swung my gun to the closest vehicle, only sagging against the car when Max got out. They'd arrived, and I could cry, but I didn't. Enzo was scaring me. Max surveyed the scene and must have seen the progression of my thoughts clear on my face because he rounded the car and held me back from launching myself between Enzo and Ivan.

I strained against Max's hold, in need of action, to assure Enzo that if Ivan harmed me, I would retaliate immediately. I would use every knife I had on me to carve him up. He didn't deserve a quick death.

Ivan took a step back, laughing in that twisted way of his. "Not too long now, Sofia." Then he was in one of the black cars and pulling away.

That was it. Max released me, and I raced around the car and launched myself into Enzo's arms. My legs wrapped around his waist, and I shivered in his embrace. He held me tightly, his face pressed into my neck as he inhaled deeply.

"We need to get you out of here," Max said.

I clung to Enzo, not wanting to let him go. He had been too close to Ivan. That asshole was crazy. He needed to die. "You should have killed him. What could they have done?"

He leaned back enough so that our eyes met and held. "War, Sof. It would be war, and a commission would be called. Not only that, but I would be defying a direct order from my boss."

"He's your father. He would understand."

"You know it's different. There are circumstances where I can defy an order. This was not one of them. A shoot-out on the road isn't something I can't handle. We both did without any problems."

Anger took over, and I scowled at him. Letting my legs drop, I pushed from his arms then smacked him on the chest. "Don't get that close to him again. If you do, I'll end him myself." I whirled on my heels and stomped back to the car, needing time to deal with my overwhelming emotions.

I squinted at the vehicle Max had exited. There was no one else inside. He hadn't brought Lil. I didn't know why I thought he would. I needed to talk with another girl. I hoped she was at the house, but she'd married into the Caruso family, so probably not. She would have wanted to stay with her grandfather, Vincenzo. They had a lot of time to make up for, and that part of the honeymoon gift from Max to Lil was time spent with family. The honeymoon had been delayed several months, but he had delivered on his promise to her.

I pulled at a thread that hung from my shirt. I would have to fix it. Enzo said a few words to Max then got into the car beside me, giving us some privacy and waiting until we were ready to go.

"I'm mad at you." I couldn't keep it in. Never could with him.

"I know," he said softly.

I turned toward him, confused by his reaction. I wanted a fight.

"The thought of Ivan anywhere near you is sending me over the edge. I don't know if I can hold back next time."

"Well, you did shoot him. Not a fatal wound, but I'm sure it hurt. Bet that felt good."

"Not good enough." His knuckles were white from how hard he gripped the steering wheel.

I sighed, letting go of my warring emotions. It wasn't helping. "I'll be careful. He had his fun. I'm sure he'll go away and regroup for whatever sick game he plans to play next."

"We shouldn't have come. It's much easier for him to get close to you here. If we were home—"

"I would have snuck out. Let's face it, Enz. I'm not good at staying where I'm supposed to. It would have felt like a prison. My brothers would have done something to drive me crazy, no matter how much I love being around them, and I would have found a way to ditch my guard."

He drew me close again, and I rested my head on his chest. "You're my everything, Sof. I can't lose you."

Chills raced over my arms. "You won't. Promise. I'm a hell of a lot tougher than I look. My brothers ensured that." And they had. "Brutes, all of them."

Enzo chuckled, and warmth filled me at the sound. "Let's go."

After he and Max exchanged a few words, the entire entourage surrounded us, and we were off and flying down the road. I twisted my hands in my lap, unable to stop fidgeting. "Where is Lil? I didn't get a chance to ask Max. So much happened, and I-I don't know, I guess—"

"Are you okay?" He studied me, concern pulling his lips into a tight line.

"Yeah, I guess."

"Lil will be at your family's house. They already planned to be there when we arrived. Are you doing all right?"

I smiled at the concern in his voice. "I am. It's not the shoot-out but the way Ivan reacts that has me unsettled. He didn't even flinch when you shot him. I would have expected something—a flicker of pain, of awareness. I mean, when you guys take a bullet, you're angry. There wasn't any emotion. That's not normal."

"He's not normal." Enzo pushed out a breath. "I can't believe I'm asking you this because it's wrong on so many levels, but what has Katya said about him?"

And that was it. I think that was why I was so disturbed. "That he likes to break women. I can't remember the specifics, but that was the gist of it." With the psychological games he was playing, I got the feeling that was his foreplay. It made me sick and very concerned about what would happen next. I wanted Enzo to kill him. I wished he had back there.

I firmed my resolve. That was on me. I didn't need Enzo to do it for me. I should have ended Ivan, not waited for someone else to pull the trigger. Screw the orders and the fact that he was an underboss to the Russian mob. He was a threat that needed to go away.

The tug on my ponytail snapped me out of my dark thoughts.

"What's going through that head of yours, Tink?"

"Oh, no. You did not call me that." Laughter bubbled up, and I smacked his hand away. He grinned, and I was transported to all the times he would tease me when we were young. It was a good memory. He'd always been sweet.

"You're missing that Tinker Bell skirt you used to wear every single day until it disintegrated, but... you've still got that look about you this morning. I think it's the ponytail."

I rolled my eyes. "God, I forgot about that phase of my life. Good times."

He snorted. "For you, maybe. You made your brothers and me sit in front of the TV and watch *FairyTale: A True Story* over and over again. Then you'd lecture us about how fairies were real and that we needed to be more careful when we played in the woods."

"Yeah." Warmth filled me at the memory, and I laughed. "I was a bit fanatical about it."

"You think?" He turned to me, that sexy-as-hell grin curving his mouth.

My heart skipped a beat. "I still have the fairies. I've never taken them down."

"I couldn't believe we found that shop when our moms took us shopping. I thought you were going to pee your pants."

"I about did. That was the coolest store—all those fairies. And they were so pretty."

"You wanted every one of them. I thought you were obsessed before, you know, with the movie and the skirt, but that place… do you remember the fit you threw?" He chuckled, and my cheeks heated. "It was legendary. You scarred Trey for life."

"I was young." Crossing my arms over my chest, I tried to block the embarrassing period of my youth when I'd thrown an Emmy-worthy fit. "Mom banned me from the store for a month. She refused to take me and told the entire household I wasn't allowed until I could act appropriately."

"I think you cried for days. Your brothers and I couldn't do anything to get you to stop."

"Until you showed up with one of those little fairies from the store." It was a tiny doll, about the size of my hand, with long brown hair and delicate wings. He'd said she looked like me and that he had to buy it. "I think I slept with that doll for a solid year."

"So worth it. You were back to your normal self right after and even played our war games with us again."

I tilted my head, observing him. "Why did you care about that? My brothers liked the break from me. I mean, they were great about including me, but there were times I drove them nuts." I grinned. "More often than not."

"You weren't so bad. Unless you got dirt on one of your skirts or whatever you were wearing. Your hair could be a complete disaster when you were little, but if anything happened to your clothes…"

"I was a holy terror. Yeah, I get it." It was true. "You never answered my question. Why did you want me playing war games with you guys?"

Enzo pulled in front of the house my family owned in Milan and threw the car into park before answering. "I liked having you around. We'd always had a connection, and then there was the blood oath not long after."

"Oh, right." Our gazes met and held. My pulse kicked up a notch from the fierceness of his expression. Power crackled around him, and I had to work to suppress a shiver at the memory of the night we'd shared.

"I'd always thought of you as mine, even when we were young. When you were around, I felt settled. It was weird, and I didn't understand it, but even then, I knew it was something special." He shrugged. "I wasn't going to fight it. Then the shooting happened, and all I could do was try to save you. That's all that mattered. Everything else sort of faded. The screaming. The blood. The men firing. I had to get to you and hide us. I can't explain it any other way. We're meant to be together."

I launched myself into his arms. I had to—he'd said the most romantic thing I'd ever heard. He cupped the back of my neck then pulled me back enough to brush his lips across mine. It quickly turned into a deep hunger as he increased the pressure, and I opened for his kiss. Heat pooled low, and I buried my fingers in his hair, tugging the short strands in a desperate attempt for more.

A loud rapping sounded against Enzo's window, and we broke apart. The world snapped back into focus, and I realized what we'd done. It wasn't safe to make out in the car. We were out in the open and needed to get inside.

"Let's go, Romeo." Max's voice caused that muscle along Enzo's square jawline to pulse. He was irritated, most likely at himself.

I sighed and got out of the car. It was a momentary lapse. We would do better. Enzo grabbed our bags from the trunk, and I met him at the entryway.

The door swung open, and Lil immediately pulled me into a tight hug. Her floral perfume and familiarity surrounded me. She pulled back enough to check that I was okay then drew me inside. The guys followed on our heels. Her long white-blond hair fell in loose waves around her shoulders, but it was the glow to her skin and in the sparkle of her blueish-purple eyes that got me. She was radiantly happy, and I was so grateful to Max for saving her. Her father, Benito Brambilla, the Mafia boss, was a complete asshat. After her mom was murdered, he'd done nothing but make her feel unloved.

Enzo passed, trailing his hand down the curve of my back before circling to my hip. He drew me into his body, and I tilted my face to his. He brushed a kiss on my forehead, and I flattened my hand on his chest, fighting against curling my fingers in the fabric of his shirt and holding him to me.

When he released me and followed Max into the kitchen, I took a minute and disengaged from the spell he'd woven with a simple touch. Tearing my gaze from his retreating form, I refocused on Lil. "How's your honeymoon going?" I went with her into the family room, and we fell onto the couch while the guys were probably getting wine or something stronger.

"What was that?" Her hand curled around mine in a firm grip, a mischievous smile playing around her lips.

I laughed, letting myself feel how happy I was with Enzo. "Exactly what you think." I winked but didn't want to talk about me. I asked her again about her honeymoon, and she took the hint.

"Incredible. I couldn't be happier." Lil smiled, but it dimmed quickly. "What's going on with Ivan?"

It was my turn to deflate. "He's scary as hell. Give me a normal enemy, and it's not that big of a deal, but him… I think he's a psychopath. I mean, there's something beyond freaky about how he's playing with me."

"How's Enz holding up?"

"As good as can be, I guess. He's worried. So far, I've been able to convince him to stay in Italy. I know it's not the best idea, but I want to witness my line's release this first year. You know? There'll be others, but this is my debut."

"I get it. You've worked so hard for this. If I were in your shoes, I would fight to be there too."

The guys came back in with wine, and we moved on to happier topics, like what Max and Lil had done on their honeymoon and how she was getting along with her grandfather, with whom she'd reconnected after the Benito fiasco.

It wasn't until an hour later, when my lips felt dry, that I realized my purse was still in the car. When I mentioned where it was, Enzo had one of the guards retrieve it. As soon as the guard handed it to me, I pulled out my lipstick and reapplied.

"Where is everyone?" My family was supposed to be there, and it was way too quiet, which meant they weren't. I needed them with me for my debut, especially Mom. Throughout my career's unfolding, the years of clothes obsession, and as each new design took life, she'd been enthusiastically by my side.

"They're on their way. The jet landed a little while ago," Max answered.

I took a glug of my wine because I needed it then swiped an excess drop from my lips. "Oh, you guys, I loved your house so much. That pool…"

"It's amazing, isn't it?" Lil grinned. "I didn't want to leave, but we'll be back a couple of times a year, I hope."

Max pulled her close, and the heated look they shared warmed me even more. My lips tingled, and I rubbed them together, thankful that my hair was up. It was getting hot in there.

Max picked up my free hand and toyed with my fingers. "Sof liked it so much that I have my lawyer speaking to the local real-estate office to see if any houses go up for sale."

I would have leaned into him, but I was sweating all of a sudden. Still, the sentiment behind looking for a house because I said I loved it there was incredible. Lil was beaming. I let myself enjoy the possibility, even though I was unsure what our outcome would be. There was still the matter of the contract and Elena. Lil didn't know. It was between Enzo and me. I'd sworn him to secrecy, refusing to say where she was.

"I hobe is…" *What the hell was that?* My lips weren't working right, and my tongue felt weird, heavy and swollen.

"Sofia." Enzo grabbed my shoulders. His eyes were wide and panicked. I glanced at Lil and Max. They were okay. I'd only had one sip of wine. It couldn't be that.

"It's not the wine," Max said. "We're fine."

"The lipstick." Lil leapt to her feet, rummaging in my purse. She pulled it out and slapped it on the table while Max yelled for the guard.

I jumped to my feet and rushed to the bathroom with Lil on my heels as Enzo made a phone call. I knew who he was calling, and I only hoped that Trey would get there soon.

After scrubbing the lipstick off with a soapy washcloth, Lil ushered me to the kitchen, where Enzo yelled for us. He had a bottle of Benadryl. And… that would put me to sleep.

He tipped the medicine to my lips, and I guzzled it until he took it away. "Twey?" He knew who I meant.

His face was like granite, but I understood why. He was

worried. I was too. It had to have been Ivan. He'd gotten to me again and right under our noses.

"Yeah, your brother thinks it's an allergic reaction. He's ten minutes out but didn't want to take a chance on it getting worse. He said to use Benadryl until he gets here."

I nodded, and he drew me into his arms. Everyone was silent as we stood there until Max returned.

"The guard that brought your purse in said there wasn't anyone at the front entrance when he went out. There were supposed to be two men there. We found them behind the bushes, unconscious. When one came to, he'd gotten a glimpse of who knocked him out before he could react. The description matches Ivan."

I tuned them out after that. My entire body was shutting down from the large dose of medicine. My knees buckled, and Enzo swung me into his arms. We were on the couch, and I was in and out of consciousness when my family arrived. Trey poked and prodded my mouth, taking a swab off the inside with a Q-tip that he put in a small plastic bag. He took the lipstick too.

"I'm going to the hospital's lab." Trey's voice drew me from sleep again. "I'll know for sure in an hour, but I have a feeling its penicillin. Sofia's allergic to it. The reaction fits."

When he left, taking the swab and lipstick with him, Enzo cradled me closer, and I let myself fall asleep, safe in his arms.

CHAPTER SEVENTEEN

SOFIA

The Benadryl took two days to wear off. My brain was foggy, and I'd missed the first day at the venue. Because of that, Mom had called in an old friend to run a few of the behind-the-scenes things. She called the models and confirmed times, and hair and makeup would soon be underway.

Trey had said I would be back to normal soon, but I wasn't feeling that way yet. I hoped he was right and it would be soon.

Good thing it was a laid-back morning of hanging inside with my family. I was annoyed, but I guessed I just wasn't meant to be at Fashion Week on the first day. At some point while I was sleeping, Trey had come back from the lab with news that penicillin, which I was allergic to, had contaminated my lipstick. It seemed Ivan the asshole had gotten into my medical records and completely screwed me over on my big day.

We needed to do something about him, and soon—he was playing too many games at my expense. Dad had already been in contact with Yuri, the Bratva boss, and Ivan's dad. Both had agreed war wasn't something they wanted. At least they gave that statement lip service. No one ever knew the Russians' plans.

The gist of the conversation was that Yuri would call Ivan back to Russia, which would be the end of it, but that wasn't likely—Ivan was having way too much fun. My brothers, Enzo, and Max all agreed that he had to die. I had no argument in his favor. One less asshole to worry about was fine with me.

If I hadn't been so scared, how worried Enzo was would have been endearing—like a rabid dog with his target just out of reach. I needed the day inside, anyway. Mom helped get everything organized and ready for the day's show. People she knew would be there, including other designers and industry professionals.

Eva had called yesterday. She was in town, having fun, but promised to be at the show on time.

It was a new day, though, and my designs would finally be out there. I couldn't wait. Security would be tight, and it would be a small miracle if Ivan were able to get in. It wouldn't be impossible, but he would have to try pretty hard.

My phone rang with a FaceTime alert and when I glanced at it my heart soared at seeing Em's name. With the phone held in front of my face, I answered it. "Em!"

"Hey." Her dark-red lips pulled in a wide grin. "Are you excited for the show? I can't believe it's happening."

"Yeah, it's surreal. I wish you were here, but I'm glad that you're safe. Things are a little… crazy."

Her dark eyes narrowed. "What's going on? Are you okay? Should I fly out?"

"No. I'm totally fine, and I'll tell you everything when I'm home." It was so good to see her face, hear her voice. She was important to me, and I hadn't realized how much I missed her being there for such a big moment in my life until she called. I felt immensely better. "Thank you for calling, Em. It's crazy right now, but I'm so ready for this."

"I know you are." Her voice softened. "You're going to do amazing."

"Are you ready?" Mom asked as she swept into the room.

Mom said "hi," and then I wrapped up my call to Em, nerves churning in my stomach with the nearness of my debut. I chewed on my bottom lip, surveying the rack of clothing that would go with us, mentally ticking through a list in my head.

"Stop." She tapped my chin, and my gaze shot to her.

I grinned and shrugged. "Habit."

"Hmm." The corners of her mouth twitched. "This is everything?"

"Yeah, I can't think of anything else that I could be missing."

"Boys!" she yelled. "Come here and help your sister."

I let her direct them, my nerves getting the best of me. After they got everything out to the vehicles, I surveyed Mom. Her dark hair was swept up in an intricate braid. Diamonds dripped from her ears and wrist. Her makeup was smoky but also not too much. It was clear that age hadn't diminished her beauty. And she towered over me, which made me frown.

"I know what you're thinking." She laughed. "There is nothing wrong with your height. You're above average. Perfect."

She pulled me into her arms, and I sighed. "I mostly don't care. But tonight, I'm worried I'll be the shortest person there."

"You're a designer and also fooling yourself if you think every one of the others is tall. I know more than a handful of designers who are shorter than you." She held me at arm's length. "And why is this a problem? Is it that you're nervous? Because you don't have anything to be anxious about. I've told you your line will be a hit, and I know what I'm talking about."

She winked, and I laughed. Mom did many things superbly, but winking wasn't one of them. She couldn't do it. The other eyelid would also attempt, and she looked like she was drunk. Funniest thing ever, and we all teased her about it, which was why she had done that.

"Thanks, Mom." I grinned, the prior butterflies gone. *I can do this. I was born to do this.*

Marco strolled in then leaned against the doorjamb. "Enzo is freaking out. It's the only good thing about today."

Mom and I turned and glared at the same time, our arms crossed.

Trey paused in the doorway and shuddered. "God, you two are frighteningly similar."

"What do you expect in a household overrun by testosterone?" I shot back before shifting my attention to our oldest brother. "What's up with Enz?"

Marco shrugged. "You'll see."

"Great." I knew what I was going to face soon, a repeat of what happened when he came into The Coffee Stop after I'd talked with Katya. I did have to admit, though, when he went all alpha, it was sexy as hell—annoying but also hot.

There was a buzz about my entrance into the fashion world. The exciting meet-cute between Mom and Dad when he literally saved her during a shoot-out while she was on the runway hit the papers and magazines in anticipation of her return with her daughter entering the world of clothing design. Paparazzi, Instagrammers, and influencers would be a nightmare as her story was romanticized all over again. We were ready. It would be a miracle if the day went off without guns.

Heads down, Mom and I double- and triple-checked everything then got in the cars with everyone else, including an entourage of guards. Some from our family had flown over from Chicago, and the rest were Sicilians. No one wanted the Russians to mess with one of ours. Security were in suits with white button-down shirts and ties, while anyone backstage was in all black. I was feeling pretty good about the day. Maybe the event would go smoothly without any of Ivan's horrid games.

Deep in my bones, I knew I wouldn't be so lucky. It was as if I could feel him breathing down my neck.

Traffic was crazy, but we got there. My brothers and Dad took everything into the designated area. The guards cleared a path so that no one could get close to us—we made an entrance. Enzo wouldn't leave my side, which posed a problem when I had to go into the back room where the models would get dressed. Mom helped. Enzo was posted at the entrance closest to where I would be, my brothers on the others, and guards at the rear door to the place. Mom and Dad were in the audience, and they had more soldiers, including Max and Lil, keeping an eye on things. I felt confident that Ivan couldn't get in. Someone would spot him.

Eva arrived not too long after we did. Lil's cousin was a force, and I enjoyed watching her boss the other models around while I was busy handling the ones that would take the runway first. I swapped a belt on one, checked for smeared makeup, and motioned for my assistant to keep an eye on them as I went down the rest of the line with a critical eye. The energy backstage was infectious, and my heart pounded in anticipation for our turn.

We had an hour until the show started, and the buzz from the crowd added a layer of excitement for all of us. I refused to let my nerves get the best of me. Everyone was ready.

Then it was time. Anticipation filled the air in an electrical current. Loud music pulsed through the venue. It was impossible not to get caught up in it.

Enzo wove through the throng of models, makeup artists, assistants, and designers until he was by my side. I paused in the tuck I was stitching on a seam under the model's arm where the bust was a tad loose. The model sucked in her breath at the sight of him, but I ignored her. He only had eyes for me.

His hand went to my waist, and he bent to my ear. "I wanted to wish you good luck."

Then his lips grazed across mine, and I sighed into him. "Thanks."

We separated, and the loss was immediate, but he pointed to the entrance on my left, murmuring that he'd be over there in case I needed anything. He would be watching, making sure nothing went wrong and that no one who shouldn't approached me. As he moved to the background, I released any worry over what could happen outside of the runway, as it was fast approaching.

I needed to change into my dress. My collection centered on the fall season, high-end attire from pants paired with heels and buttery-soft tops to cocktail dresses then to evening wear. And the best part was all of them had hidden pockets that did not hinder the lines. The models at the start of our runway walk would wear the most casual outfits before we moved through the collection and ended with evening attire. Eva was last, and I would follow her in my black A-line gown with plunging neckline.

Finished with the models, over whom I swept one last critical eye, I went to change. We had only minutes before we were on, and I needed to hurry. I didn't know where the time had gone. Mom took my place while I slipped into a room my family had segregated for our use only.

Once dressed, I returned, and Mom squeezed my hand, her red lips in a knowing grin. After I walked down the runway at the end, I would return for a few words with Mom by my side— I couldn't have done it without her.

When it was my turn, we were ready, and the models took to the catwalk. I couldn't have hoped for a better reception. I'd instructed the models to line both sides of the runway, with the first and last ones who had originally taken the stage at the front of both lines. When I stepped out, my black gown swirled around my legs. A rush of adrenaline surged. The lights glared from overhead and flashes flickered as I glided to the end of the runway. I paused, smiled, then turned and headed back, the models falling into line behind me in a choreographed maneuver. I was on cloud nine.

The rest of the evening was a blur, and I was riding a high

from how well my designs were liked. Eva was on cloud nine. The dress was a huge hit, and I swore it was because she'd worn it. That woman had attitude. She gave it the right amount of sexy danger, and the crowd ate it up.

After talking with so many people, it was hard to keep them straight. Mom introduced me to those she knew and who would be beneficial to my career. That alone was incredibly exciting—I had a career.

Throughout everything, Enzo stayed by my side. He'd gotten many interested looks from women and several from the men. My brothers were eating up the attention, but no matter what, everyone in my family had that cold glint in their eyes. They were watching, and it gave me a sense of security for which I was immeasurably grateful.

A light tap on my shoulder had me turning. Jasmine, one of the models, told me Eva needed to speak to me. I made my way to where she'd indicated. I spotted her toward the back corner, near the area where we'd gotten ready, which worked for me because I had to use the bathroom. I slipped into the room at the back we'd commandeered. It had its own bathroom, which was a plus. I needed a quick change into my deadly pants with the weapons and a fitted black T-shirt. When we left, we had a route that would avoid the press, so I didn't need to be in anything fancy.

Enzo continued to be my shadow, except for when I went to get changed and use the bathroom. Last I saw of him, he was waiting near the entrance to the main dressing room. That was a mistake. He should have come in with me. As soon as I set foot outside of the bathroom door, a large form loomed over me. I think my heart stopped in recognition just as Ivan's hand clamped over my mouth.

It wasn't the end. I wouldn't let him win. One scream, and an army would be on him. I stomped on his foot with my heel. I palmed one of the knives from my weapon-designed pants—the longer one—and plunged it into his leg. When his arms loosened, I wrenched myself away then kicked the blade. It buried to the hilt, sticking out the back.

He didn't make a sound, and that freaked me out most of all. My gun was in my purse, and I pulled it out, dropping the bag to the floor, and opened my mouth to scream. His fist came at me before I could squeeze the trigger. Pain exploded on the side of my head. Everything went dark.

CHAPTER EIGHTEEN

SOFIA

I awoke with my head pounding and chills all over my body. I took shallow breaths to keep the bile inching up my throat to a minimum from the aftereffects of Ivan's punch to the face. My stomach convulsed, and I gagged. It was the wrong thing to do. I knew better, but my body wouldn't listen.

"You're awake."

The deep, heavily accented Russian voice made my skin crawl even more. Everything that had happened in the bathroom flooded my mind in an overwhelming couple of seconds. *How had he gotten to me when the place was crawling with Italian Mafia?*

As I screwed up and couldn't fake being unconscious, I peeled my scratchy, dry eyelids open. I was sitting up, not lying down. Dizziness had made it hard to determine my position.

My head hung down, and the first thing I glimpsed were my bare legs. The fucker. That was the reason I was so cold. He'd stripped my clothes off, except for my black bralette and panties. I hoped he had a hell of a time getting that knife out of his thigh.

A hollow laugh left my lips as I smelled the faint odor of

burning flesh. He'd had to cauterize his wound. *Good.* I bet it hurt. In slow increments, I lifted my head, despite the way my neck muscles screamed in protest. I sat with my arms tied behind me and my ankles secured to the chair's legs.

Without telegraphing what I was doing, I took in the size of the room and any defining features within to help for when I was untied and could escape. The chair was wood, not metal. I didn't think there was much space behind me, as it appeared to be a small area, about ten by ten, give or take, with one window to my left that had dusty old blinds covering it. A nondescript light fixture was above us, which meant we were probably in the center of the room, and my estimate of size was correct.

Wherever he'd taken me, I got the impression it was way off the beaten path and not in Milan. I only hoped that my cell phone was with me or that Enzo had slipped a tracking device into my clothes. Speaking of those, I would need to find out where they were.

It was time, and my gaze locked on his. He sat on a chair opposite me. A table was between us. On it was a bottle of vodka and two shot glasses. Interesting. We took each other's measure in that initial look. I let him see steel and cold hard determination in mine. He would not break me. I knew what he wanted, and I would take Elena's secret to the grave if necessary.

He had a brutish rectangular face. Honestly, he reminded me of a hammer. There was nothing soft about him. I would never understand why Eva thought he was handsome. He terrified me. Then there were his eyes, the windows to the soul. In my life, I'd seen dead eyes, but his were twisted and empty, another reason I thought he was a psychopath.

He splashed vodka into the shot glasses before he set the bottle back on the table. He lifted one and downed it. The other, he turned a few times before bringing it to my lips. I wasn't going to turn it down and didn't fight him. I welcomed the burn as the alcohol slid down my throat.

A smile toyed with his firm lips, then he brought my glass to his mouth, sliding his tongue around the edge where mine had touched. The warmth from the alcohol dissipated. I feared for what he would do to me because tasting where my lips had been wasn't a good sign.

I wanted to push him to find out what he had planned, but that was probably the worst idea. It was better to keep things neutral. "How did you get us out of there?" It had to have been difficult.

He poured another shot for himself. After he downed it, a sinister smile curved his firm, thin lips. "It was easy. Italians showed up the day of but not the one before."

My stomach sank. *Do they know who took me?* They had to have, but I had a feeling that no one had seen us. "Fine. You were there the day before, hiding somewhere. How did you get us out?"

"I had a few Bratva on the inside. A double garment rack rolled past the bathroom, pausing long enough for me to slip in the middle of it without being noticed. The clothes shielded us from prying eyes. Two of my men were left behind to start a fight and detract as Mikhail rolled us out of there, up the ramp, and into the waiting van. Right under the noses of the ones meant to keep you safe."

I gripped my hands tightly behind the chair, where he couldn't see my desperate attempt for control. It was so simple. Someone should have checked the garment racks. I studied him in silence. There was more to the story. I could tell in the amusement dancing in his light eyes. Maybe he would share more later. I wouldn't ask again because I didn't think I could keep my voice from revealing more than I wanted.

"For now, we drink together. Get to know one another." He poured two more shots, and despite the revulsion at knowing his tongue had been where my lips had been, I accepted the alcohol when he put it to my mouth. I needed the liquid courage for what was to come. My guess was that it would be a long and unpleasant night.

The pain would come soon. I welcomed the burn of the vodka, willingly accepting a third shot. The chill of the room faded, replaced by a false warmth from the alcohol. I shouldn't have, but I hoped for another.

"I wonder why Katya chose you." His legs were sprawled out beneath the table while he toyed with his shot glass. With his index finger, he tilted the small cup, twirling it on its edge.

"Chose me for what?" I scrunched my eyebrows, feigning a question. I had practice denying plenty of things. *The* Call of Duty *video game of Marco's that I tossed in the garbage? Wasn't me. The gray hoodie Nico loved but was the perfect material for a cute pair of sleep shorts? No idea—and no, I'd bought the shorts I was wearing. Trey's new super-soft pajama pants? I did not put those in my room. It must have been someone else's mistake.*

Ivan wouldn't get anything out of me. My brothers had perfected torture—maybe not Ivan's brand, but enough for me to draw strength. Not once had I broken. When Mom and Dad caught my brothers during an interrogation, I got my show, complete with popcorn and their punishment, which was worth it.

"Katya was in Chicago a day before I arrived four years ago. My spies tell me that you went for a run with Elena. Later that day, she was gone without a trace—at least then. I know better now. And I could have gone after Nicole Caruso when she learned her daughter was missing. She was inconsolable with fear, with grief. It appeared genuine."

"I remember that when Elena's clothes were found in Italy and brought back. There was so much blood."

His gaze flicked from the glass to mine and remained. The lack of emotion inside the light orbs chilled me to the bone.

"There was blood, yes. But death? No. I've come across evidence that was sadly overlooked. A recording at the train station showed you with another woman."

I snorted. "So? I have lots of friends. The last time I saw Elena was when we went for a run."

"It was Elena. Same shape. Same walk. The hair was different. The clothes. It was her."

"Your logic has holes." I needed to keep him talking as long as possible because when he stopped, things would happen that I wouldn't like. "And have you asked these questions of Katya? She works with your family. I have no idea why you think she would come to me with anything."

He slammed the glass onto the table. "She works for my family but not always for the right members of it. Katya is… different. I have not asked her directly."

"Maybe you should?" And she could kill him for me. I would have paid to see that.

"After our little… talk." His cold gaze ran the length of my body. "Are you comfortable?"

"Very much so. I do wonder about my clothes and why you took them. I'm concerned about the answer, but I have to let you in on a secret. They won't fit you."

Ivan grinned then rapped his knuckles against the table. "Interesting pants. I'm familiar with them and the secrets they hold."

Oh no. Does that mean he found Elena? They were the same general design she was wearing when I helped her leave and go into hiding. I smirked. "You got intimate with my pants? Okay then. To each his own."

Ivan stood then rounded the table and leaned against the edge. He ran his finger along my cheek, my skin crawling the entire time, but I schooled my features—no reaction. He wanted one.

"Elena's death will be much swifter than yours. I won't enjoy playing with her." He gripped my chin, squeezing it until I looked at him. "You are lovely, but you won't be when I'm finished with you."

He removed my large hoop earrings and the diamond studs that were in my second piercings with surprising gentleness then moved behind me and slipped my rings from my fingers. He placed each item on the table in front of me. I didn't want to consider why he would remove anything with metal from my body, but I knew the reason. God, I knew.

This is going to suck. And I still didn't understand why he wanted Elena. Keeping him talking was my best bet. If he wasn't, he would do things that I wished he wouldn't. "Who is Elena to you?"

A dark storm gathered in his eyes, and my heart skipped a beat, threatening to stop altogether.

His lips peeled back, and I witnessed the first glimpse of what I thought was emotion. "She is a loose end."

CHAPTER NINETEEN

ENZO

My fingers wrapped around the Russian Bratva scum as I slammed him against the wall in the room where the models had gotten ready. We'd cleared the place out, except for two men. "Where is she?" I yelled into one man's face, inches from mine and turning purple. Panic flared in his bulging eyes, and he wheezed what little air filtered through his closing windpipe.

I tightened my fingers, unable to control how much I wanted to make him suffer. As his mouth worked like a fish's, Trey's voice penetrated.

"Let him go." Hands curled around my biceps, pulling me off the guy.

With a roar, I lunged forward. I wasn't finished.

Trey got in my face. The others, whoever the fuck they were, jerked me back a step. "We need him alive," Trey growled.

I snapped out of it enough to hear his angry words. Our gazes locked, and I read swirling outrage mixed with fear in his, which must have matched mine. It was easier to feed the fury than face what could have been happening to Sofia.

In my peripheral vision, Sofia's Mom and Liliana stood with their hands clasped and tears streaming down their pale faces. Seeing their pain and worry only pissed me off more. *This never should have happened.*

"If you kill him, we might lose any hope of finding her." Trey's hands gripped the lapels of my suit. "Get it together. Do this right."

I gave him a single nod. He'd gotten through. Trey motioned for the two holding me back to let go. The Russian stood before me, gasping. I removed my jacket and rolled up my shirtsleeves.

I unholstered my gun, jammed the barrel into his shoulder, then pulled the trigger. He grunted, his jaw flexing. I duplicated the wound in his other shoulder then shoved him into a nearby chair. Blood ran from both injuries, staining his white shirt red. I stared into his bloodshot eyes, wondering how long it would be until I broke him. He was part of Ivan's plan. He had to have at least an idea where Sofia could be.

I notched my head in Trey's direction. "He's a doctor." Several weapons, including a few we'd removed from the guy, were nearby. I picked up a wicked-looking serrated blade and slid it from its sheath. "That means whatever damage I do to you, he can patch you up enough to keep you alive." I shrugged. "And if you pass out from pain or blood loss, there will be no reprieve. He'll bring you back to consciousness so I can do it all over again."

The edge of the blade was against his throat. I applied a small amount of pressure, tipping his chin up. Our gazes met. The whites of his eyes were rimmed in red. Blood trickled from his mouth and the cut on his swollen lip from when I'd hit him a few times. "You know how this knife will feel, so there's no need to explain the damage I can do. You can save yourself, or we can spend some time together." I ran the blade along his forearm, drawing blood in its wake. "I'm hoping you choose option number two."

Marco zip-tied the guy's wrists to the chair's armrests before turning back to the second one we'd detained. The fact that two Russian soldiers had breached our security did not sit well. Trey, who'd prepared for any catastrophe by bringing extra medical supplies, came in behind Marco and got a makeshift IV started. The Russians weren't going to give up information easily. I caught Marco's gaze. The savageness I felt reflected at me before I refocused on the soldier I held a knife to.

There was nothing I wouldn't do to find Sofia. It was only a matter of time.

Sofia

Ivan left me to think about my lack of response about Elena's whereabouts. It was cold, and with only my bralette and panties on, I had goose bumps all over my exposed skin. He'd taken off all my jewelry, and while that eased my mind regarding his intentions about removing my clothes, it also confirmed what he planned to do next. There wasn't anything on me that contained metal. When he came back… it would suck.

Three soldiers had been in and out of the room, bringing equipment. A hook was added to the ceiling and a rope dropped on the table. Next, a bucket of water was left, followed by a jug of the same. Then a black bundle was placed not far from me on the same table, untied and unrolled. The sight of the different blades and pliers were enough to make me want to cry and throw up on the spot. I would do neither. There were places in my mind where I could hide.

Once they'd brought everything in and set it up, the soldiers left, shutting the door behind them. Time moved slowly, and my anxiety was a live wire inside of me, fine-tuned to every little noise.

Another half an hour passed before Ivan showed up. I did my best to appear unaffected, rearranging my features to reflect indifference, while terror took root in the remembered voice of Katya's comment: "He likes to break women." The phrase played on repeat, foreshadowing what was about to happen.

Ivan didn't sit on the opposite side of the table that time. Instead, he stopped at my side, waiting. When he said nothing, I tilted my head to look him in the eyes and judge what he was thinking. A crooked grin hovered around his mouth, which was in no way sexy. It was frightening. Dark intent sparkled in his light eyes, and every muscle in my body tightened for what was to come.

"I'm feeling generous." His thick finger traced the edge of my jawline, and I fought my reaction to pull away. "All this"—he swept his hand around the room—"can stop if you tell me where Elena is."

"I can't tell you what I don't know." Inside, I was shaking, but I was still. My voice was strong. I would not give him anything. Already, I could feel my mind retreating. I had to survive long enough for Enzo to find me.

Ivan rubbed his meaty hands together. "Let's begin, then." He wheeled a cart over then put a leather strap between my teeth. He wore rubber gloves, the thick kind, as he sparked the conductors in front of me, heightening my anxiety. I knew what I would feel at the first touch and as volts of electricity passed through my body.

Dad had made sure we trained in ways to survive torture. Mom hadn't liked it, and they'd fought. I know she cried every time we went into the basement, where we had a soundproof room and way too many dangerous instruments. At the time, it had been a nightmare. But I understood why he taught us to resist pain, and in that moment, I was grateful.

The first touch of the metal to my body made every muscle lock up as I convulsed. That was when I slipped deep into my mind. Electrocution sucked. I zoned out in between sessions. He removed the leather from between my teeth then questioned me. I repeated that I didn't know anything. We had evidence that she'd died in Italy. Over and over again, he continued the process—shock then question.

It didn't take long until my body was screaming, and I was barely aware. He must have left the room because nothing horrible happened. Still tied to the chair, I let my head fall forward and closed my eyes, unable to hang on any longer. I sank into welcomed unconsciousness.

A sharp pain ran along my arms, from my wrists to my shoulders, as I jerked awake. I wasn't sleeping in the chair. My arms were strung above my head by the hook Ivan's lackeys had installed. I dangled from the ceiling, balancing on my toes. Everything hurt, and it was about to get so much worse.

Ivan circled me, a cricket bat dangling from his hand. "Where is Elena?"

"Dead. Her body burned in a building in Italy." I'd repeated that so much I was beginning to believe it myself.

The crack against the back of my thighs had me seeing stars. I sagged against the ropes, and they cut into my wrists, but I managed to keep the scream inside, my teeth instead sinking into my cheek. Blood filled my mouth. *How long will I last?* Nausea churned in my stomach, and my body shook, making it harder to remain on my toes and keep my full weight off my rope-bound hands.

"Where is Elena?" His voice jolted me to stay with him when all I wanted to do was slip out of consciousness.

"I told you." I gritted my teeth, forcing myself to repeat the same statement for the hundredth time.

The next crack struck the back of my heels. I cried out. Tears leaked from my eyes, and blood trickled down my arms from where the rope tore the skin. I hated it for many reasons—the pain, yes, but most of all how I was present with him, unable to retreat into my mind, and the way he made me scream.

His fist struck my kidney. I was near blacking out again, but he waved smelling salts under my nose, stopping me from relief. Over and over, he repeated the same question, for which I only had the one answer about Elena's whereabouts: six feet under. She was dead.

I didn't know how long I hung there until he released the tension, and I fell to the cement floor in a heap. The rope remained around my wrists, and I curled into myself in case he kicked me. Seconds passed before he left the room with a slam of the door.

Desperate for relief, I traveled to my most cherished memories and sank into it. I was in junior high. Two years older than me, Enzo was in high school and had come over to watch the game or something with my brothers. I couldn't remember why because all I cared about was that he was in my house and I might see him, talk to him.

I'd checked a few times, and the four of them, Enzo and my three brothers, were engrossed in whatever game or fight they were watching, yelling at the TV as if they were a part of what was happening. Not wanting to be in there, I headed to the screened-in porch with a few magazines. I was flipping through the pages when he appeared at the door then leaned against the frame.

"What are you doing?" He pushed off the door and came in before sitting next to me. I swore my heart would fly out of my chest. His arm came around the back of the love seat glider, and he eased closer to see the pages I was flipping through without comprehending what I saw.

"How's Monica?" I couldn't help myself from asking about his girlfriend. *Is he still with her? God, I hope not.* I hated her on principle.

"Gone. Not important." He toyed with a portion of my hair, and inside, I sighed. He was single again. All was right in the world.

I rested against him, and he pushed the glider so that it rocked back and forth. We would sit that way when it was just the two of us, and I loved being so close to him. His other hand cupped the side of my face and turned me toward him, and tiny flutters of awareness traveled through me at the contact. His eyes were stormy, dark, and very sexy.

Then he leaned close, and I felt his breath against my lips. We were separated by less than an inch. My heart slammed against my rib cage, threatening to break through. That close, I could see the gold flecks in his eyes. He held himself still, waiting. I could only think it was for me to tell him to back off. I wouldn't. Then he closed the distance, and his lips brushed across mine once, twice before he nipped on my lower lip. His tongue soothed the spot, and my lips parted. Fireworks exploded with each caress. When he kissed me again, I moaned.

He tangled his fingers in my hair and tilted my head to deepen the kiss. When he drew back, my pulse was out of control. Nothing existed but how he held me, touched me. Finally, my dreams had come true, and Enzo was mine. He pulled back farther, and I scrunched my brows in confusion before I heard Marco calling for him. Enzo lurched to his feet as Marco came around the corner and filled the space that separated the porch from the house.

"What are you doing? The fight is about to start."

I was going to kill my brother. He just didn't know it yet. Marco's gaze darted from Enzo to me then back again. Something dark infused his features, and Enzo hurried to leave with him. He turned once, regret on his face and a parting of "I'll talk to you later, Sof" leaving his very kissable lips.

Enzo, I would forgive. Marco, I would not.

It was my first kiss, one of many Enzo and I would share.

Lying there on that concrete floor, I let my body relax further and enjoyed the trip down memory lane, effectively taking me away from the very messed-up situation I was in. It wouldn't last. I knew in my heart that Enzo would come for me. He always had.

CHAPTER TWENTY

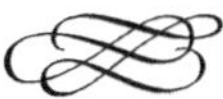

SOFIA

Light pierced my eyelids, and I blinked groggily. Ivan was back. Every twenty minutes or so, he woke me. Sleep deprivation sucked, and my body was a mass of pain. It was another torture technique I was familiar with, and while I hated it, I would take it over other methods every single time.

"I enjoy your fight." His heavily accented voice jarred me the rest of the way to consciousness, the light doing the initial duty.

"I've got a lot of that. No need to worry."

He chuckled. "This will stop once you tell me where Elena is."

"Really?" I blinked slowly at him as he hovered over me. "I'm to believe you'll let me go if I lie to you? If I make up something about a dead woman being alive?" A sadistic laugh tumbled from between my swollen and cracked lips. "That contradicts your personality."

Ivan grabbed my face, squeezing painfully. "Don't think that you know me."

Seconds later, he left. The bruising would remain, but I didn't care any longer. I had my memories. I would relive them rather than dwell on my current plight. They would see me through the darkness. Sifting through several, I returned to my first kiss. I traveled back to that moment again. Enzo hadn't left that night without seeking me out again.

His dark hair fell across his forehead when he found me later in the kitchen, getting a glass of water. "I've wanted to do that for so long."

Heat stained my cheeks as I thought about the kiss. I set the water down, waiting. I wanted to ask him if it meant I would be his girlfriend now, but I knew the answer. He'd reacted to Marco coming after him. Risking their friendship didn't seem likely, and my brothers would be pissed. Instead of asking, I went to him, wrapping my arms around his waist and letting him hold me. We stayed like that for a long time.

Blinding light yanked me from Enzo's embrace. I was confused, teetering between the past and the present, clearly wanting one over the other. I tried to shield my eyes with my bound hands, but Ivan pulled them taut over my head, stretching my body along the cement. I took note that my ankles were free. Contracting my stomach muscles and ignoring the pain in my side and the back of my thighs, I lifted my legs to a pike—straight and at a ninety-degree angle—then wrapped them around Ivan's head, pulling down hard. Knocked off-balance, he tried to correct and leaned toward the hold he had on my wrists, listing to the side.

The fight was short-lived. He grabbed my neck and slammed me back to the ground. As his fingers tightened, I gasped. Dilated eyes bore into mine, and I had a sense he enjoyed what he was doing. Dark spots converged on the edges of my sight. He blurred before me. My limbs were heavy, and my lungs were starved for air. The pressure on my airway lessened. When he finally eased off my neck, I gulped oxygen down my burning throat while tears streamed from my eyes.

"This is good. It keeps me on my toes." Ivan grinned. "Now, tell me about Elena."

"That she's dead?" I glared at him, furious that he'd found that entertaining. I couldn't give up. I had to try to escape on my own, but the last thing I wanted to do was increase his enjoyment. I'd have to wait for a sure way to strike. There would be an opening, if not that time around then the next or the one after that.

He drew the chair near me, the wood scraping against the cement floor as he did so. I didn't like the proximity of his feet but didn't move away or curl into myself. Elbows to his knees, he leaned over me. "I've seen the footage of you with her at the train station. There is no denying it. Where did you send Elena?"

"I didn't send her anywhere. The last time I saw her was when we went jogging. That was it. There was no train station with Elena. Nothing. Someone took her from us, and it wasn't me."

"You'll give in eventually, and then I'll have what I want." Ivan stood, scooted the chair back, then left the room. The door shut with a click, and the sound of a lock slammed home.

Once again, it was dark, and I breathed a sigh of relief. Things could have gone much worse. I was thankful he didn't have a strobe light and loud music playing or my eyes propped open and forced to watch whatever messed-up thing he displayed with all the rest of the stimuli happening. Knowing he would be back with another round of sleep deprivation activities, I sank back into my mind, where I knew Enzo would be.

Lil, Em, and Marissa had been my best friends when I was young. That circle expanded to include Elena and Eva, but I was closest with Enzo. We had an unbreakable bond. That first kiss had led to others. Always in secret, or so we'd thought.

Enzo came over regularly, and we found every opportunity to be together that we could that year. Once when he was over hanging out with my brothers, there was another game on TV. When he could, he slipped away to use the bathroom but went to my room instead. I wasn't surprised to see him. He stepped over the threshold then shut and locked the door. His dark eyes smoldered, and butterflies erupted in my stomach. The textbook fell from my hands. He took it, moved it to my nightstand, then sat next to me. I went to him willingly. In his arms, I came alive.

"We don't have much time, but I can't stay away."

I knew the feeling. There was nothing better than being in his embrace. His lips pressed to mine. My body was hypersensitive to his touch, and I edged closer, winding my arms around his neck and flattening myself against him. His mouth slanted over mine, deepening the kiss. In his embrace, I let go of all control, trusting him to keep me safe.

His hands dropped to my hips, and he lifted me so that I straddled his lap. Heat spread through my body as his hands moved up and then cupped my head. He made me feel cherished, sexy, and loved. When I wasn't with him, I dreamed about him.

In my life, I had to be my own hero. And if need be, I would. But Enzo was my hero—always.

A moan rumbled up his chest, and I shivered at the deliciousness of it. When he pulled away, breaking our kiss, I wanted to cry out. It was never enough.

His forehead rested against mine as we caught our breath. Stolen moments were all we had. But someday, we would have more. I was sure of it. His fingers tightened in my hair, and I tilted my head at his urging until our gazes met as we sat back.

"Sof." He shifted so that the pad of his thumb ran over my swollen lips. "You're so beautiful. I want more with you, but having to sneak around like this… it's not right."

Oh no. He wasn't thinking about telling them. Our families would disagree. I knew it deep in my bones. I wasn't sure why. Maybe it was the way his dad looked when he saw us together. I swore the man's expression said regret. I put my hand over

Enzo's mouth, stopping him. "Don't say anything. If you do, I have a feeling something will keep us apart."

"They probably won't be happy." He flashed that crooked grin that turned me into a puddle. "But I want to be able to spend more time with you. And not hide or sneak around like now."

"No one's stopping us from spending time together. You're over here a lot."

"You know what I mean, Sof." He kissed me again, and I didn't think of anything but the feeling of his lips on mine.

My body jerked from a physical force. Panic flooded my system, severing my connection to the past and thrusting me into the undesirable present. Ivan shook my shoulders while light infiltrated the torture room.

"Where is she?" he repeated.

"Dead," I croaked. My throat was dry, my body slow to respond to my commands. But my mind… that was something he would not break. We went over the same questions for half an hour. Then two soldiers entered, one to hold my feet and the other to keep my arms over my head as I lay back on the floor. They waterboarded me. They held my jaw open and flooded my mouth with water, slowly drowning me, only to release me in the last seconds. Only then was I given a reprieve on my side to cough up the water forced down my throat. The questions would start. The same question, over and over again. When I didn't give a satisfactory answer, the process began again.

My answers never changed. If they had, he would probably have killed me. Even if he didn't, if I told him, Elena would be dead for real.

"Sooner or later, you'll be desperate enough for me to stop this. Then you'll tell me what I want to know."

Ivan's face was close to mine. Too close. I didn't like it. He lifted a strand of my hair and gave it a sharp tug.

"I'm enjoying our time. I'm not an impatient man. No one

will find us here. We can spend hours, days, even weeks together without the risk of being discovered." He buried his hand in my hair and fisted it, forcing my head up and our eyes to meet. "Did you enjoy the roses? They were originally white. I soaked them in blood for you. We'll watch this pretty skin of yours painted in rivers of red."

"You're wrong," I managed between teeth that chattered. "Enzo will come for me, and if he doesn't, I'll end you. I'll cut you from dick to chin."

"That's very visual."

"You'll be dead soon." I would make it happen. I didn't care if he was Yuri's eldest and second-in-command. He was not untouchable after having done all he had to me.

"I see you've had time to think about me. And while I enjoy the way your mind works, if you harm me, you will bring war down upon you from the Russians, one you will not be able to win."

"That's interesting, as you've harmed me. You've already started the war." I pointed out the obvious as he threw back his head and laughed, releasing the tight hold on my hair. My scalp continued to scream in protest.

"We can stop, Sofia, just as soon as you tell me where Elena is."

"Why is Elena so important to you? A loose end from what?"

His sick laughter filled the room once more. "It's amusing that you don't know who she is." His fist crashed into my jaw, and the world blinked out once more.

CHAPTER TWENTY-ONE

ENZO

age was my constant companion as we sped along the highway, closing in on the safe house location the two Russian soldiers had given up. It'd taken a lot longer than we'd hoped to extract the information. Max took one and I the other. By the end, my guy had a busted knee, gunshot wounds in his thighs and shoulder, broken fingers, arm, and several ribs, and multiple contusions. Both were barely alive when we dumped them on the doorstep of the Bratva Brotherhood.

The fact that they had a presence in Italy was grating but convenient to send our message. We hadn't killed them, a kindness we would use to our advantage—because Ivan would die. Our mercy with the other soldiers was to show that it wasn't our goal to go in and kill him despite the dire circumstances. It was our endgame. But we were hoping our actions with those two indicated otherwise.

The house was on the outskirts of town in a rural area, a tad run-down. Five cars followed as I increased the speed past what was safe. *Please be alive.* Sofia was my life. The connection we'd had since we were kids was stronger than ever. I couldn't lose her. If she were gone, I would be lost. There would be nothing left.

Max rode shotgun in my car, but neither of us said a word. Talking wouldn't help. We had Glocks and machine guns within reach and a trunk full of more weapons, should we need them. Sofia's brothers and father were in the car directly behind us. Five minutes out, and my hands tightened on the wheel. There was little chance of surprising Ivan when we pulled up, as armed men surrounded the small house set into a hillside.

The soldiers took aim as we barreled down the road. I counted six to start. Max lowered his window as gunshots shattered the windshield. While he fired out of the passenger side, I aimed out the front. The car bumped over the edge of the driveway. I kept my foot on the gas until we were near the front then slammed on the brakes. We skidded to a stop then leapt from the car.

The soldiers behind us joined the gunfight. Two men fell. Then three. The fourth ran toward us, a grenade in hand, only stopping when a small hole bloomed in his forehead. He crumpled to his knees. The other two near him dove away, and we braced for the explosion's impact.

The grenade detonated, the sound deafening. We lost hearing as we slammed the cars into park and poured out of the vehicles, guns strapped over our chests and in both hands. Neighbors were a good distance away. They were insignificant on my radar. A dozen soldiers emerged from the vehicle behind ours. If there were problems from the Russians outside or the neighbors, they could deal with it.

Every muscle in my body was tense. My jaw clenched, and I ground my teeth. The need for Ivan's blood called to me, impossible to deny. Max was on my six as I kicked in the front door, both my guns drawn and leading the way inside. It was dark. The shades were closed, and very little light filtered through the windows. My hearing returned, only a slight residual buzzing, but that would soon be gone.

I paused for half a second, listening. Nothing. *She has to be here.* I felt her. We'd always known when the other was near. My ears strained for the slightest sound. A slight scuff and I jerked to the side, grunting, as a bullet slammed into my shoulder instead of my heart. Max and I unleashed a volley of fire. Sofia's family did the same then split down the opposite hallway to search the west side of the house. When a body hit the floor, landing partially in front of Max and me, we paused, again listening as we crept forward.

It was the place. We were running out of time. The Russians we'd captured at Sofia's event would have been dropped off to the Brava, and the Russians would come to enforce. The clock was ticking.

Max whirled. Shots rained on us, and I covered his back. Two soldiers converged on us. They came from another part of the house, circling to take us unaware. Didn't matter. They would die too. My leg jerked, and I looked down. A bullet had found its mark. Not lethal. It slowed me down but didn't stop me. It hadn't hit an artery.

Blood splattered as Max and I unloaded everything we had from our 9mms into the two men. When they fell, I looked over Max. He'd taken a hit to the arm. We turned as one. I was drawn to that section of the house as if my heart beat in sync with hers, and I followed the faint drum that beckoned.

The sound of gunfire traveled through the house as her brothers and dad continued to clear the rooms and eliminate the men Ivan had there.

We edged down the hall, one foot in front of the other. Time slowed as we crept closer to where I knew he held Sofia. Then I saw it—a bolt lock on the door at the end. Ivan had to have been in there with her, waiting. Ready.

As soon as we entered the room, we would be vulnerable. I didn't care. I would give my life to ensure Sofia was safe.

I signaled to Max, and he moved to the opposite side of the doorframe. Then I shifted, faced the door, kicked it open, then dropped. I slid in feet first. Images came in frames—a snapshot of time. Max joined me, going to the right while I went left. We were in. Consecutive shots fired. From Ivan. From us.

Ivan was near the left corner with Sofia, wearing only her bra and panties, using her as a human shield. Tears streamed down her bruised face, but her eyes were fierce. I read her intent. She wanted him dead. We were on the same page. Max shot his leg. I tagged his shoulders. Sofia was too small to hide behind.

Cold fury directed my actions. Every inch of Ivan I could shoot, I did. The burn of returned fire registered, but I kept going. Sofia's eyes flashed. I knew what she was going to do. I gave a signal for Max to wait. She went limp, her head lolling to the side. Enough space was there to strike at his heart. I took aim, squeezed the trigger, and hit my target.

Ivan stumbled. Max knocked the gun from Ivan's hand. I reached for Sofia before she, too, hit the ground. Our men swarmed the room. Someone offered a Mylar thermal blanket they must have gotten from the triage kit one of the soldiers had brought. I draped it around Sof's shoulders and hugged her to me. She looped her bound hands over my head.

"Sof—" My voice cracked as she lay her head on my chest, a tiny sigh escaping her parted lips. The emotions were over-whelming, but I had a job to do. Clenching my teeth, I shoved everything I was feeling aside and focused on what needed to be done.

We only had seconds left with Ivan. A gunshot to the heart didn't mean instant death. It was slightly off-center to ensure Sof wasn't hit. Red pumped from the hole. Soon, his brain would starve from lack of oxygen as his heart ceased pumping blood through his body. His blood pressure was rapidly falling, and a fogginess filled his light eyes. We needed information quickly.

"How did you find Sofia?" I growled the question with her clutched against my chest. He had appeared in too many places —across the street from her studio on North Michigan Avenue and in the coffee place nearby. Those could have been garnered from observation. What would have been harder information to come by was the location of Max's home in Mondello and the fact that we'd flown out earlier than planned. There was no answer from Ivan—he was fading fast. I shook his shoulder, leaning closer. Sofia was too close to him, but I refused to release her now that she was back in my arms.

"How did you find her?" I said between clenched teeth.

Sofia turned her head from where it was pressed against me, facing him. Her hoarse voice cracked when she asked, "The house? The roses? How did you find me?"

His eyes focused for a second on her and a cruel grin curved his lips before falling away. "You have a rat."

"Who?" My voice thundered, bouncing off the walls in the small room. Ivan's laugh was a wet gurgle then no more. He was gone.

I kicked his side, unable to stem the surge of frustration and rage at the situation. Slowly, the contents of the room trickled into my consciousness. I'd been so focused on Ivan and Sofia that I didn't scrutinize all he'd done to her. There was a hook in the ceiling. The rope around her wrists registered, as did the electroshock machine in the corner, a jug of partially full water along the wall, and the drain in the center of the floor. *That motherfucker.* I wanted to shoot him all over again.

It was time to pull out. Trey needed to look over Sofia. Max and I were also losing a lot of blood. After double-checking that Ivan had no pulse, I stood on shaky legs with Sofia clutched to me. One of the guys told me to hold up as he cut the rope from her wrists. Ivan's blood pooled around his body and inched closer to my feet. Sof moved her arms down, tucking her battered wrists under the blanket. I backed up and pivoted out of there. Her brothers and dad rushed into the room, but I wouldn't let her go.

I nuzzled her ear, breathing her in for just a moment. We didn't have a lot of time, but my heart didn't get that memo. "I love you, Sofia." Her eyes were at half-mast. "Stay with me, please."

Her fingers curled around my shirt as I lifted her in my arms to carry her out of there. "I love you, too, Enz. I knew you would come." Her voice was whisper-soft and filled with pain.

She was all that mattered. I needed to get her to safety. The Russians would be swarming the place soon.

Max motioned for one of our soldiers to come with us after Trey did a quick check for any urgent injuries that Sofia had. Once he motioned we could drive back to treat her, the soldier got behind the wheel, Max took the front passenger seat, and I got in the back with Sofia on my lap. Her head rested against my chest. She sagged against me, twitching now and again as tremors ran through her.

I wanted to know everything that happened. My hand rubbed her back, eager to touch every inch of her, reassuring myself that she was alive, that she was safe. I'd thought the day my sister was taken was the worst, but I was wrong. This was so much worse. I'd never felt the kind of fear as I had when I discovered Sofia was missing. And I would make sure I never did again. She was my world, and I was determined to protect her at all costs.

CHAPTER TWENTY-TWO

ENZO

As much as I wanted to whisk Sofia away and have her all to myself, I knew her family would not be okay with that. Then there were her injuries. Her brothers and father had raced back to the house, getting there before we did.

The car came to a halt in front of the house Sofia's family owned in Milan. As soon as we opened the doors, her mother ran out, tears streaming down her face. Robert, her father, wrapped an arm around his wife, giving me space to stand. When he went to take Sofia from me, I gave a single shake of my head. I didn't trust myself to speak. She had passed out in the car and was unconscious, and I was terrified something was wrong that I couldn't see.

They waited until I headed for the front door then followed me. Her brothers crowded inside. My progress was slow, and I could tell they wanted to tear her from my arms to hurry the process of patching her up, but I couldn't let her go. It was physically impossible. I couldn't release her.

Max was somewhere behind us, as were several of the men who needed their injuries looked over. Marco led us to one of the guest rooms. The others were directed elsewhere. Max must have gone with the soldiers, as only Sofia and I were with Trey. She was his top priority. Mine too.

Thick blankets and sheets covered the bed. Trey motioned for me to put her on the makeshift exam table set up in the center of the room. When I lay her down, she didn't stir at all.

"Sit down before you fall," Trey ordered.

"No." I didn't want to leave her side.

"Christ, Enzo." Trey's head snapped up from where he was examining the bruise around her side. "I need to focus on my sister, and you're bleeding all over the place. Sit the fuck down so I don't have to stop what I'm doing to help you when you pass out from blood loss and crash to the floor."

"Awesome bedside manner," I grumbled but did as he ordered. He had a point. While sitting, I watched his every action. He was pale, and his voice had broken when he'd first told me to lay her on the table. I understood what he felt, his helplessness and the fear at seeing his sister wounded.

He started an IV for Sofia then told me he would remove it later after all the fluids and the one shot of antibiotics he'd inserted into the line were administered.

"Nico!" Trey yelled. "Get me the ultrasound machine." Her parents and brothers had been hovering then rushing to help the others, only to return with the same lost expression we all wore while Sofia lay there unconscious.

"What are you using that for?"

Nico rolled in a cart that had several pieces of equipment on it and a laptop. "How is she?"

Trey didn't turn as he answered his brother. "Asleep. Her pulse is good. I haven't had a chance to assess anything else."

Nico nodded then went to help in the other room. Trey booted up the ultrasound then squirted some gel on her side. He moved the wand over the bruising while watching the image on the screen. Trey pointed to the picture of her kidney, and I leaned forward.

"I wanted to make sure her kidney wasn't damaged. It looks fine but will be sore from how he hit her." He checked a few more places then sterilized everything that needed it. He cleaned and bandaged her wrists. She stirred but went back to sleep after her unfocused eyes settled on Trey then me.

He addressed the small contusions then turned to me. "She'll be okay." His voice cracked again, and he took a moment to run his hands over his face, shielding his eyes. "God, Sof." Bending at the waist, Trey inhaled slowly before regaining control. When he straightened, his mouth was set into a grim line. "She probably hasn't slept much, which is why I'm not concerned over her being so out of it. When she wakes, I'll reexamine her and give her a mild sedative. Right now, she needs sleep to help the recovery process. Let's get your wounds patched up, and then you can carry her to her room, where she'll be more comfortable."

Trey made fast work of my injuries, including digging out a bullet lodged close to a bone. The pain was a dull ache in the back of my mind that raced with what I'd seen in that room and the thought of everything Sofia had gone through. The rest of the bullets had gone through or grazed the side of my body. He applied shower shield protection over the bandaged areas so I could get cleaned up when Sofia woke. She would want to scrub every inch of herself, regardless of how painful the process would be. I planned to be right there beside her to help.

"Get Sofia settled." Robert stood in the doorway. Marco joined his dad, a grave expression on both their faces. "We need to have a meeting about the Russians."

"She's ready." Trey went over by her side, slipping his hand into hers briefly before he locked gazes with me. "I'm grateful that you saved my sister. But if you hurt her, I'll be coming for you. We all will."

"I wouldn't expect anything less," I said before standing and carefully tucking a blanket around Sofia then gathering her in my arms. I paused at the doorway. "I'm staying with her. Fill me in about the meeting. I just can't..." My voice broke at the end, and I closed my eyes, taking a moment to regain control. She was safe. I had to deal with the emotions that were bubbling to the surface about what could have happened and what did.

"I'll let my dad know." Trey slipped past me and headed to the other room to stitch up Max and anyone else who needed attention.

Angela, Sofia's mom, placed a hand on mine and squeezed. "Follow me." She led us through to the back stairway then down a hall before going into one of the upstairs bedrooms. "She stays in this room when we're in Milan." She pulled back the covers then turned to me. Tears flooded her red-rimmed eyes, and exhaustion reflected in the weariness that shadowed her features. "Thank you for bringing my daughter back to us."

I lay Sofia on the bed, tucking her in before drawing Angela into my arms. She broke down, her thin frame shaking like a leaf. "Nothing would have kept me from her. Not anymore."

She drew back, and I released her. "It's about time, Enzo." A watery smile curved her mouth and brought a touch of sparkle to her eyes, but the stark fear couldn't be fully distinguished. "Stay with her and let me know when she wakes, please, or if you need anything."

I promised I would then shut the door with a soft click behind her. I needed a shower, but I would take one once she awoke. Toeing off my shoes, I slipped under the covers with her, drawing her into my arms. The feel of her did so much to soothe the savage side of me that wanted to go to the Bratva's doorstep and slaughter every last one of them.

I buried my face in the top of her head and inhaled. A puff of air on my chest reassured me that she was breathing, and I let my body relax in slow increments.

Every now and again, a soft knock sounded at the door. Trey took her vitals and removed the IV once the bag was empty. Then Nico came in and kissed her forehead, not saying a word. Her parents checked in, smoothing her hair and brushing kisses over her forehead. Lil hugged her while I held her, burying her face in her hair and crying until Max came in and drew her away. When Marco came and sat on a chair he'd pulled next to the bed, I waited. He had things to say. They were written all over his face.

"Yuri has been informed. He was… furious. Retaliation was his first reaction until everything that Ivan had done was disclosed and confirmed by the Russian presence here. We orchestrated a virtual conference. Things are up in the air, precarious. We'll likely go to war with the Bratva Brotherhood, but we're doing what we can to prevent that."

"Bring it on. I'm ready." The need to spill their blood roared inside me.

"Frank Rossi has been brought into the loop, as well as Stefano. With his daughter Camila there and married to Yuri's only living son, that causes an issue. Things are escalating, and we have to fly back to Chicago. A meeting is scheduled in three days from now between all the bosses then with Yuri afterward. That's all the time we were able to give you and Sofia." He leaned back in the chair, his eyes closing briefly.

"Thank you for that. I want to take her back to Max's villa and let her recover for a day or two before we fly back."

Marco nodded. "I know she would like that. The jet will be here and ready for your return home."

Sofia stirred, and everything in me stilled. Seconds passed while Marco and I held our breaths, waiting. When she didn't open her eyes or move again, I refocused on him. There was still the issue of Elena, and while I wanted to let Marco know, I needed to discuss it with Sofia first.

"My dad, Max, and I were talking about what the Five Families need going into the future. It's a conversation Max and Stefano initiated a while ago, if you remember."

"I do." It had transpired when we came together to help Max recover Lil after her abduction. Max was already boss, and Stefano, Marco, and I were second-in-command and in-line. From what Marco was saying, his father must have agreed and would soon step down. I knew my father would be like-minded. Stefano's father was a whole other animal.

"I'll let you get some rest." He stood then left the room, the door shutting softly behind him.

A few hours passed, and I must have dozed on and off because when I opened my eyes, it was to the sight of Sofia's amber ones locked on mine. A shudder ran through me at the mixture of love and pain I read in her. "How are you feeling?"

"Much better now that I'm with you." She rested a hand against the side of my face. "Thank you for coming for me."

"I'll always come after you." I brushed a clump of hair behind her ear, wanting to trail my fingers along her smooth skin but wary of the bruising. The last thing I wanted was to cause her more pain.

"Ivan?"

"He's dead. We can talk more about it later."

She nodded, relief momentarily relaxing her taut features. "I need a shower." Her eyes misted, and the pain overrode any other emotion visible in her expression.

I got out of bed, motioning for her to wait a minute. She rolled to her back, wincing slightly, then stilled. I called her mom, let her know she was awake, and asked if she would have someone change the sheets. Sofia wouldn't want to lie back on them after she washed off the traces of Ivan's handiwork.

Then I lifted her into my arms and carried her into the bath-room, shutting the door with my heel. I set her on her feet, making sure she was steady before I leaned into the large spa-like shower with a rainfall showerhead, another handheld one, and multiple jets. I turned on the overhead one and adjusted the temperature. No jets. Then I got to work removing her bra and panties. She shuddered, and I wasn't sure if it was from my touch or finally getting out of what she'd worn while Ivan had her. I tossed the garments into the garbage. I didn't need to ask. I threw my clothes on the floor. Her mom had anticipated a shower and must have slipped in while I dozed because there was a small pile of clean clothes for both of us on the sink's counter.

With my arm around Sofia's waist, we stepped into the shower and under the water. She sighed and flattened her hands against my chest then rested her forehead there. I grabbed the soap and lathered a sponge before running it along her shoulders, moving her hair to the side, then doing the same to her back. When she lifted her head, I went to work on the rest of her body, making sure to gently clean every inch. Next was her hair. I took my time working with the long, thick strands. The conditioner was last. While it coated her hair, I guided her to the bench seat in the shower. She sat, and the conditioner did its thing while I quickly washed. I rinsed her hair with the handheld showerhead. Her eyes were closed, and she looked like she was seconds from falling asleep. I needed to get her back into bed.

I shut the water off then helped her to stand on shaky legs. I toweled her dry then got her dressed in soft sleep shorts and a matching pink top with "Pro Naps, Anti Pants" printed on it. I could get on board with that too. There were gray sweats for me, which I pulled on. Sofia sat on the makeup chair, and I picked up a brush. I started at the ends of her long, dark hair and worked through the knots carefully. Once her hair was combed out, I grabbed the blow-dryer and went to work. Soon, her hair was dry enough that it wouldn't bother her to lie down.

I lifted her back into my arms, and we left the bathroom only to be greeted by her family, Max, and Lil.

I got her situated then stepped back enough to let them gush over her. Ten minutes later, her eyes were drooping. Everyone took their leave for the moment, and I climbed back into bed, pulling her into my arms. She snuggled into me and was asleep in a matter of seconds. I followed. I would go anywhere she did.

The next morning, when Sofia woke, we spent a few hours with her family. They needed the time with her before flying home to Chicago. We had two days before we had to return. It was time we both needed, and I could tell she was relieved. The house was locked up, and we got into one of the cars in the garage and drove to Mondello.

In yoga pants and a soft long-sleeved pale-pink tee, most of her bruising was hidden, except what was on her face. Makeup helped to camouflage it, but not enough. She'd thrown an old ball cap of one of her brother's on her head and a large pair of sunglasses that covered half her face. No one would question her or stare. She was going with a blending tactic, and I totally got it. Recovery was the goal for those two days, not stress and not paparazzi.

It wasn't long until we were parked in front of Max's waterfront home in Mondello. She sighed as soon as we entered, a look of contentment sliding over her. "I just want to hang poolside today."

I went outside with her, pulling a lounge chair with cushions closer to the pool but still in the shaded overhang off one section. She lowered herself and relaxed back while I carried over a small side table and a seat for myself. Then I placed two glasses of water on the table before I dropped into the chair next to her.

"How are you feeling?" I threaded my fingers with hers, needing the connection.

Her head rested against the backrest, and she gazed at the rippling pool water. "Physically, I'm sore, but it'll pass. I'm not too worried about that."

I waited. Something had clearly disturbed her, which wasn't surprising. When she didn't say anything more, I brought up the meeting and the discussion between her brothers and father. It would affect all of us, and I knew she would want to hear it. I told her about the shift in leadership that would take place soon but probably not until we resolved the Russian crisis. There would be blowback from Yuri, but we would have to see how that played out.

"I want to be closer, Enz." She shivered, but it was warm outside. "Can you move the table to the other side?"

Worry for how quiet she was being quickened my movements as I did as she asked then thought better of the setup. There was one of those round couch-bed things with lots of pillows and the canopy over half of it. I rearranged everything, got her situated on it, then joined her. The tables were on either side of us, within easy reach. I lifted my arm, and she scooted over so that her head rested on my shoulder. I held her against me. That was much better.

"Do you want to talk about what happened with Ivan?" It took everything in me to speak calmly. I wanted to rage about him laying a finger on her and kill him all over again, more slowly.

She released a heavy breath. "I don't want to rehash it all. I just want to move past it. There's something to be said about growing up in the world we do. At least it prepares us and helps to process and compartmentalize things."

Her fingers toyed with the hem of my shirt then slipped underneath to lie flat against my chest. "There's something else we need to go over, and it can't be swept under any rugs." She tilted her head back and met my gaze.

I said what I needed to, bringing up the matter she wanted to discuss but seemed hesitant to. "Elena. The fact that she's alive and what we're going to do about her."

When she rolled her lower lip with her teeth, I gently tugged it free. She was worried, and I hoped she would share why.

"Are you asking about Elena because you're going to have to leave me?"

"What?" I hadn't even thought about that. The contract... I would have to find a way to deal with that soon. "Never. I've already told you that you're stuck with me. We made this decision. I won't go back on my word, Sof. And I can't imagine my life without you in it."

"Okay. Good." Her voice was soft, exhaustion riding the words.

"We still need to figure out what to say about Elena, though."

I wasn't prepared for the way her eyes hardened or the flash of worry that sliced through the amber. "We're not going to *do* anything. Where Elena is hiding and that she's alive is not my secret to reveal. When we're back in Chicago, I'll get in touch with Katya."

"The hell you will." I rolled her on her back, looming over her. The thought of the assassin coming anywhere near her threatened a heart attack. Determination lit within her gaze. She hadn't seen firsthand what the assassin could do, and I didn't like her being within a mile of the Russian. I feared that Yuri would dispatch Katya, and when Sofia reached out to her, I would lose the only woman I'd ever loved.

She flattened her palm against my chest, soothing the thunderous pounding. "You'll be present when I call her and if I have to meet with her."

I smoothed her hair back, trailing my fingers along the curve of her cheek. I couldn't let her anywhere near Katya, not without being there too. "Promise me, Sofia. I don't think I can handle anything happening to you. I love you. You're my world."

Tears misted her eyes, and she nodded. "I promise. I love you too."

CHAPTER TWENTY-THREE

SOFIA

We'd spent the day before by the pool, lying on the round daybed with the canopy and alternating between talking and dozing. Enzo wouldn't leave my side unless he got something for me: a blanket, food, whatever I wanted. Honestly, I only needed him, and he gave me that as well. We hadn't come inside until close to eleven at night and only because it was turning chilly and I was beyond tired. A storm raged during the night, but only for a short period, although it was possible that I slept through a lot of it.

The smell of coffee permeated the air, drawing me from a deep sleep. The bed was so comfortable that it was hard to imagine getting up, but I needed to. If I didn't, there was a chance I would hide from the world, making it harder to rejoin it, and that wasn't me. Ivan would not break me. He hadn't when he'd held me captive, and the experience itself wouldn't either. I wouldn't let it.

Light spilled into the room, and I could hear Enzo moving around in the kitchen, getting breakfast ready. If I didn't get up immediately, I knew he would bring it to me—he was that attentive. It was fantastic, but I needed to retake control of my life.

In slow increments, I threw the white duvet off, gingerly sat up, then slid my legs over the side of the bed until my feet were on the floor. I made my way to the kitchen to behold the sexiest sight ever. I had to pause to take him in.

Enzo had a spatula in hand and was dishing scrambled eggs onto two plates that already had bacon on them. He'd set the island with coffee, napkins, and silverware because he got me—he knew I would want to get up to prove to myself that I could, but he wouldn't utter a word about it. God, I loved that man.

"Morning." He put the frying pan and spatula down, placed his hands flat on the island, and leaned forward. Gray sweats rode low on his hips, his muscles flexed and rolled as he moved, and my mouth watered at the sight. But it was his eyes and the love shining in them that slew me the most.

"Morning," I murmured, working hard to control my desire for him, especially with how I was feeling. I pulled out one of the stools as he rounded the corner then sat. "Thanks for making breakfast."

"Hmm, of course." He brushed a kiss across my cheek before digging into his food.

I did the same—devoured it, actually. I hadn't realized how hungry I was. When I finished, I pushed the plate away then leaned back in my chair, my gaze drawn to the patio. Enzo had opened the doors, and the soothing sound of the waves and the scent of the sea filled the space. "I love it here. I wish we could stay longer."

"We have all day." He got up with our dishes and took them to the sink. "Is there anything you want to do? Hang by the pool, go into town, or watch a movie?"

My body ached. Going somewhere meant I would have to do my hair and put makeup on to cover my bruises, which wasn't appealing. "Hot tub. Just an easy day."

"I'll finish cleaning up here then meet you out there."

His lips touched mine in a sweet kiss, and I almost melted on the spot. I could see that what had happened and how I was hurting was killing him. He let me go, and I slowly made my way to the bedroom to put on my red bikini. It always made me feel better, even though my bruises were on full display. There was no way in hell I was wearing a black one after what had happened with Ivan. I shuddered at the thought. *No, thank you.* I needed some color in my life. I changed then hobbled to the patio and gingerly dipped a toe into the water. It was hot but not unbearable, and I knew it would go a long way to ease some of the soreness.

Goose bumps danced along my skin, and I lowered myself into the swirling water as Enzo came out wearing the gray-and-white ombre board shorts I loved. He joined me, holding my hand under the water, and I rested my head on his shoulder. "How are you healing?" He'd taken a few bullets but didn't seem hindered by them. Trey had his wounds and my wrists covered with a shower shield, so the hot tub wasn't an issue.

Enzo glanced at the bandages on his chest. "They don't bother me."

I didn't expect them to. Getting shot wasn't unusual in our way of life, especially for the men. I was doing better, too, but I was still tired. I could easily have spent a week in bed, but only if Enzo was there with me.

It was a gorgeous fall day without a cloud in the sky. I loved how the infinity pool bled into the view of the sea. The contrast between the chilly air and hot water was decadent. The time there was precious, and I couldn't thank my family enough for figuring out a way for us to have that gift. We needed to address things, but I couldn't bring myself to ruin it by talking about what was coming. We would face that soon enough.

The feeling of Enzo's hard body against my side was doing

things to me only aided by the buoyancy of the water. In there, I was weightless, my injuries less bothersome.

He released my hand then slid his down my thigh. I shivered as he lifted my leg, bending it so that he could take a look at one of my very bruised heels. With the softest touch, he ran his thumb over it.

"When I see what he did to you, I want to kill him all over again but very slowly." His voice was low and hoarse.

I eased my foot back under the water when he released it, and I wondered if he'd seen the bruising on the backs of my thighs too. But then I realized how ridiculous that was. Of course he had. I must have sighed because he tipped my chin up with his finger until our eyes met. "If you were able to, I would want to participate." I shifted so that I was straddling him, my knees on the bench we were on. I rested my hand along the side of his face. "Thank you for coming for me and for killing him. I never doubted that you would. It kept me strong."

When he opened his mouth to say something, I took advantage and captured his lips with mine, pouring everything I felt into the kiss. It didn't take long for it to spiral out of control.

His hands gripped my hips in a gentle touch, guiding me down so that I felt his hard length at the apex of my thighs. My hair was piled on top of my head in a messy bun, allowing easy access to my neck. He pressed kisses on my shoulder then on my neck, and I shivered as his teeth nipped at the sensitive skin.

"I need you, Sof." He trailed the kisses higher, along my jaw then to the corner of my mouth. "I saw you tied, beaten, and abused by the enemy. I need to feel you're alive, that you're real and here with me in every way." His lips brushed across mine in a teasing caress. "That you're mine."

I lost myself in his touch, in the stark need and the love shimmering in his passion-filled eyes.

"But I need to know you're okay with this." He was holding back, every touch careful, gentle.

I was okay and more than on board. "I want this too."

That was all he needed to hear before he dipped his head, our lips collided in an explosion of desire, and all thought fled. He cradled the back of my head, angling my face to deepen the kiss. The need between us was undeniable.

Then he broke the connection and trailed kisses along my neck, and I tilted my head to give him greater access. Shivers followed in the wake of his lips as my nerve endings burst into life.

My fingers traced over the well-defined contours of his broad shoulders, the muscles flexing and shifting beneath my exploration. When I grazed his tight abdomen, I felt the quick intake of air from his mouth against my neck. He had my bikini top unhooked with a tug then trailed along my skin as he pushed the straps down my arms.

I eased back out of his embrace and stood. The chilly air caused goose bumps, and I shivered. I slid the rest of my bathing suit off then dropped it on the edge of the hot tub. I closed the distance between us, shivering at his hungry gaze as it traveled over me. He leaned forward, pressing careful kisses along every bruised inch of my side, melting my heart.

Then he yanked off his suit, and I feasted greedily at the sight of him. He was mine, and I was never letting him go.

"God, Sof. You're so beautiful." He lifted me, and I straddled him, both of us hissing at the contact.

My body hummed, hypersensitive to his every touch. The buoyancy of the water made everything easier for me, and I eased myself back, the bubbles holding me up as his hands traveled lower. I arched and cried out as he brushed along my slit. Heat pooled low, and my body softened, readying for him. The buildup of desire bubbled within me as he caressed me—I couldn't wait much longer. When his gentle touches changed to urgent ones, in sync with my escalating need, I met his burning gaze and begged him to hurry.

My fingers bit into his shoulders as he positioned us so that he nestled at the entrance to my core. Our gazes locked, and I moaned at how heated he was. I shook with anticipation, but he held my hips, controlling my body. A whimper escaped before he slanted his mouth over mine. So many sensations warred in my body—too many. Want, need, desire, and love sizzled through me, slicking the way for his entry.

His fingers traced my seam, finding the throbbing bundle of nerves desperate for his touch. When he circled the nub, applying intoxicating friction, I groaned. Then he pressed against my core, and I pushed back, needing so badly for him to fill me that I was dizzy. When he plunged inside, I exploded around him in quivering convulsions.

Each thrust sent a volley of cresting waves, and as I claimed his mouth in a heated kiss, he teased my clit until I teetered over the edge. When he whispered my name, I was done for—my body erupted, and I arched, clenching tightly around him and crying out from my release. His head fell to where my neck met my shoulder, his moan vibrating against my skin as he chased my climax with his own.

We clung to one another, shaken by the intensity of what we'd experienced. We stayed plastered to one another in the hot tub, neither of us wanting to move as our breathing regulated. When he lifted my hips and slid out of me, I whimpered at the emptiness. Then he pulled me back against him, cradling me in his arms, and I tangled my arms around his neck.

I never wanted the day to end. But it would in a few hours, and then we would have to board the jet and return home. For the time being, I would enjoy being in Enzo's embrace, my body relaxed and pressed against his, feeling content, protected, and well-loved.

CHAPTER TWENTY-FOUR

SOFIA

I ignored my suitcase and left my room, not wanting to feel trapped anywhere. It was nice to be back in Chicago, but I missed sleeping in the same bed as Enzo and having him around all the time. At least my family was there. I didn't want to stay alone in a house after my stint with Ivan. While I could handle what happened and move on from it, I knew better than to put myself in a difficult situation.

The front door slammed, and Trey called out. I hovered on the landing, unsure what I wanted to do. He would question me, all that doctor stuff. The fact that he was only a year older meant nothing in the eyes of his profession, even if he was the Mafia's surgeon—he would have outranked me regardless of our age. And even though I looked and acted like everything was okay, it wasn't. What I worried about the most was losing Enzo. With Ivan gone, Elena had an opportunity to come home.

I needed to talk to Katya, but I'd promised Enzo he could be present. Later, then. I was almost positive he would come over. *He'd better*. I missed him.

When Trey didn't come upstairs to find me on the landing, I realized he'd gone elsewhere in the house. I was halfway down the stairs when the front door opened. A familiar blond head popped into view, and I hurried the rest of the way to the first floor.

"There you are." Lil grinned, rushing over then enveloping me in a careful hug. "We've come to entertain you."

I peered behind her to find Em and Eva hovering nearby with bags. "We brought food and wine." Eva winked.

"You do realize we have a fully stocked kitchen and wine cellar, right?" I was confused.

Em rolled her eyes then looped my arm in hers, dragging me toward the media room. "Not junk food."

Eva took a quick detour to the kitchen, which Lil informed me was for glasses. I let her and Em steer me, and when we were in the media room, we sat. Eva was soon to follow. We passed around pretzels, Cheetos, and chocolate. Eva popped the cork from the wine, handed us each a glass, then got busy scrolling through the list of movies.

"We're watching *Holidate* then *Mr. Right* because they're funny as hell."

"Hell is funny?" Lil had a twinkle in her eyes.

"Um, yes." Eva waved away her comment. "I live there most of the time. I should know."

"How are you doing?" Em asked me directly.

"I'm okay. Sore, obviously, but other than that, I'm fine." I wanted to find Enzo and camp wherever he was. I did not like the separation.

Lil took a breath. "Don't take this the wrong way, but—"

"When is that ever a good way to start anything?" Em's eyebrows rose, and she pointed at me. "Look at her. Her shoulders immediately tensed."

The drama. I shook my head. "Just ask."

"Why aren't you staying with Enzo? I saw the two of you together, and I can't believe he would let you out of his sight for even one second."

I squeezed Lil's hand, because yeah, she did get it. She'd been there in Milan and had seen how we interacted. "My family would have flipped if I stayed anywhere other than here. But they also said he could sleep over. It... helps."

Eva's head reared back. "Your family is letting him sleep in the same bed with you?"

"I'm twenty-two!" I met their knowing looks and rolled my eyes when they laughed. "Fine. Not in the same bed, but in a nearby room. He sneaks in, though, so it's all good."

"He's got a place in the city. When are you going to move in with him?" Eva leaned forward on her knees, never taking her gaze off me.

"We haven't talked about anything beyond coming home from Italy. I would love another week there."

"Yeah." Lil's expression softened and turned dreamy. "That house is incredible. I could easily go back."

"How's married life?" I could tell it was good, but we hadn't had a lot of time to talk much since she'd married Max.

"Amazing." Lil pulled the Cheetos from Em's hand and snagged a few. "Did you know we're building a house not far from here?"

I couldn't help but laugh. "Pretty soon, we'll do the same. The entire neighborhood will be infected with Mafia."

Em nudged my shoulder. "When are you and my brother building a house, then?"

"Oh, right. Because we've had deep conversations lately." I huffed then grabbed the chocolate from Eva. "I'm hoping we can talk about our living arrangements soon. I'm doing better. I don't think my family would freak if I stayed a few nights at his place." I needed a change of subject because I was getting anxious. "What about you, Em? How's Stefano?"

Heat infused Em's cheeks, and she leaned back into her chair, clearly uncomfortable with the topic shift. "I have no idea how he is. I haven't seen him in a few days."

"Hmm, that needs to change." Lil squeezed Em's leg.

"Do something about it," Eva said.

Em frowned then turned to Eva. "You need to take the same advice. You told us at the lake house about how you felt about Tony. What have you done there?"

It seemed like a long time since we'd seen either Stefano or Tony, but maybe that was just me. I was sure both Em and Eva had spoken with them. My focus had been to avoid Ivan. Then there was Enzo. I leaned back in my soft leather chair, letting my friends' chatter fill the room in a happy buzz. Eva started *Mr. Right*, and I let my mind wander to what had bothered me most since waking: Elena. *What will happen when she returns home, and will I lose Enzo to a Mafia contract?*

<hr>

Enzo

I stood in the warehouse where we held commissions and big meetings like the one currently in progress. The table was full of Mafia bosses and their seconds: Frank Rossi, his son Stefano, my father, Emilio Vitale, Max Caruso and his second, Sal, Sofia's father, Robert La Rosa, Marco... even Benito Brambilla showed up. Although Benito's time was limited, both Max and I had our sights on him.

Since I called this meeting, I slapped my hand on the table, drawing everyone's attention. Max met my gaze then Stefano. We had to bring our behind-the-scenes conversation to light. "It's time for a change in leadership and to unite the Five Families to increase our strength and power."

Frank leaned back in his chair, his expression shuttered and hard. Benito slammed his fist on the table and shoved to his feet. "We are strong as we are."

"You make us weak." He'd fallen right into my hands. "Your

dealings with the cartel are causing a divide and exposing us to outsiders who will do whatever it takes to break us down. How is it that you don't see that? The cartel will not make a good business partner. They will eat you alive, destroy you from the inside out like a cancer."

Benito glanced at Rossi and La Rosa, reading the room, then chuckled. "You have a lot to learn about business."

No one was fooled. "That's one of the problems, a weak link that blocks what should be—Five Families strong."

"That's not all we need to discuss," Robert interjected. "The Russians are barely leashed from Ivan's death. Yuri sees reason, but not everyone in his family agrees. Frank"—he turned to face the Rossi boss—"have you heard from your daughter? Are you able to reach out to her?"

Camila Rossi was married to Vic, the youngest and only remaining son of Yuri Pavlov. That connection was shady, and I wasn't sure why he'd married her to the Russians, but I would have bet that Benito knew. There was bad blood between those two, and I hoped we could expose it.

"I haven't spoken to Camila since her wedding day. She will be of no help," Frank said.

From the corner of my eye, I saw Stefano's granite expression and the fury simmering there, directed at his father.

"You gained something by marrying your daughter to the Bratva. We're facing probable retaliation, and we need to be prepared." Robert leaned forward, his piercing gaze locked on Frank.

"It's Antonio who had the connection. Frank married Cami to save himself from Yuri and Ivan when a business venture went bad. The Russians don't owe him anything," Stefano said through gritted teeth.

Christ, it was eerie how Stefano had so many secrets squirreled away. And Antonio... *if only the dead could talk when we needed them.* I rubbed a hand across my forehead. I would speak to Stefano later, with Max present. It would be a miracle if Frank gave up any information. He was tight-lipped like that and not a cooperative arm of the Five Families. Neither was Benito nor Antonio when he was alive.

"It's time, Enzo. I'm ready." Emilio, my father, stood and withdrew his saint's card. He shared a look with Robert, Marco's father, and he, too, retrieved his card from the inside pocket of his suit.

As my father turned to me, shock traveled through my body. His hand fell on my shoulder in a brief squeeze. Then he withdrew a knife and pricked my finger, squeezing a small amount of blood onto the card. I swore the sacred oath simultaneously with Marco, while the edge of both saint's cards were lit, passed from hand to hand, then quickly blown out. My father and Marco's returned the singed cards to their inside suit pockets.

A sense of rightness filled me as I stepped into the role I had been destined for since birth. I was ready to lead and to fight for those I loved.

CHAPTER TWENTY-FIVE

SOFIA

I loved the movies my friends had chosen. With Em, Lil, and Eva, I'd spent the evening laughing to the point of pain, thanks to my injuries, then self-medicating with wine to numb it, rinsing, and repeating. As far as evenings went, it was a good one, and I was grateful for them.

They'd peppered me with questions about my debut at Fashion Week in Milan, and I couldn't help but feel the warm glow of success. Mom had made sure my sketchbooks were nearby, and I'd already started on the next line—just some preliminary sketches, but promising. Enzo mentioned next year's event like it was a sure thing, and I couldn't lie—it made me fall more in love with him.

Eva snort-laughed, pulling me back into the room with them and mostly out of my thoughts. I only wished it was all the way out. The movies managed to hold my interest for a few more minutes. But try as I might have, I still couldn't shut off my mind about the problems Enzo and I would face. I needed to get ahead of them so we could make an informed decision about our relationship. He'd said nothing mattered except us and that he wouldn't give me up, but there would be the matter of the ironclad marriage contract that was still in effect, despite the few people who knew—Elena, Katya, Enzo, and me.

The second movie was playing, and I whispered "bathroom" to Lil and made my escape. I couldn't wait for Enzo. It was driving me crazy. I sent him a quick message to say I was contacting Katya and promised not to leave the house or meet her without him, just in case he pulled the alpha-male card and rushed over during the very important meeting he was in with the other bosses and seconds. It was just a text. There was no reason I had to wait for him. He could read what was said later.

Down the hall, away from the bursts of laughter coming from the theater room, I leaned against the wall, pulling up Katya's name in my messenger app.

Me: *Ivan is dead.*

Katya: *He's dead. You're alive. Problem?*

Me: *Yes—war? He was their son.*

Katya: *It's probable. But—nothing is as it seems.*

Me: *YOU KEEP SAYING THAT—WTH DOES IT MEAN????*

She'd said that to Elena and me in college, and I was tired of her vague answers. I wanted some hard facts so I could make informed decisions.

Katya: *Figure it out.*

Me: **eye roll emoji.**

Me: *Can she come back?*

Katya: *Did you contact her?*

Me: *No. Thought it might not be safe.*

Katya: *Wait. Possible retaliation for Ivan.*

Me: **head thump emoji.**

Katya: *After payback, do it.*

Katya: *It's time for new blood. Things will work out.*

I shoved my phone into my pocket. That was not helpful. *Dammit.* After a few deep breaths, I went back to the theater room. I found my seat to the tune of my friends' hysterical laughter while they passed a bottle of wine around. I absently took it and refilled my glass before handing it to Lil. She leaned close, her blond hair spilling over her armrest.

"Are you all right?" Concern mixed with the tears misting her eyes from laughing.

"Yeah." I forced a smile. "Just worried about the guys."

"Oh. Maybe we should find out if they're okay? Max said it would be a long meeting and not to worry. But maybe we should? Did you hear something else?"

"No." I patted her hand. "I'm just paranoid. Ignore me."

"I'll text Max to be sure," Lil said.

"Why are you texting Max?" Eva leaned around both Em and me to ask Lil. Her eyes were wide, and if I hadn't known better, I would've thought her expression was a little panicked.

"Just checking in." Lil shrugged, answering without looking at Eva. "Their meeting is going long, and with the expected trouble with the Russians… it's smart."

"I'm sure they're good. No need to be around Max all the time." Eva tossed a popcorn kernel at Lil. "Besides, we don't want them to come here and encroach on girls' night."

"Leave her alone. She misses him." Em nudged Eva then pointed at the movie. "We're missing great stuff. We should try that."

I glanced at the screen. The main characters in the movie were tossing knives back and forth. "We sort of do that."

"Yeah, but not like that," Emiliana argued.

I watched them play with knives like it was some kind of a dance. She wasn't wrong. It was cool. "Huh, I guess you're right. Still, I'm not sure if I'm okay with any of you throwing a knife at my head and taking the chance of not catching it."

"No thanks." Eva snorted. "I'm not risking one of you crazy bitches screwing it up and offing me. I'm aware of how jealous Lil is of me, and with her shitty aim…"

I laughed, regretting it immediately as stabbing pain shot along my side from my bruised kidney, ribs, and jaw. "As if." I glanced at her and the way her leg bounced. She was too easy. "You sound worried, Eva. Something you're not telling us?"

"You're annoying." Eva huffed.

"Chill." Em narrowed her eyes at Eva. "What crawled up your ass tonight? We're joking around. That's it."

Lil's face scrunched up, but she ignored her cousin as she texted. "Max said all's good. They're wrapping things up and will be back soon." She pocketed her phone then motioned for Em to pass the wine.

We fell into silence, absorbed in the fight scene on the screen. I tried to push away the sense of foreboding about the guys being away and enjoy the movie. But I couldn't stop seeing the text from Katya screaming through my mind on repeat about the probability of retaliation. I wanted Enzo with me.

<hr>

Enzo

A sense of surrealism floated around the experience of swearing in. Both Marco and I were bosses. That altered things. I hoped in a good way. We'd talked before about making changes. All that stood in our way were Frank Rossi and Benito Brambilla. Stefano needed to lead the Rossi family, and we had no one to take over for Benito unless Lil or Max wanted to step up. If they did, we'd be Five Families strong, rather than the divided shit that went on with those two still in power.

We still had one order of business that I was determined to discuss, and I called it to attention. "We need to address the vulnerability Benito has brought to the families by striking a deal with the cartel."

Max's body stilled, and I noted that he looked as if he'd found prey and would soon strike. It was his right after what

Benito had put Lil through. I leaned back in my chair, content with Max taking over that topic.

"You have no warehouses or product left," Max said with a smirk. "It's time to end your dreams of owning the corner on the drug market."

Red infused Benito's round cheeks, and he lurched to his feet, pointing his finger at Max. He was damn lucky that was all it was, or he would have been wearing holes. "Because of you!" he roared, Max locked in his sight. "The cartel wouldn't have been a problem if you hadn't destroyed the product."

"You're aware that Vincenzo Brambilla shut it down. He forbids drugs being a part of the business."

"He runs the Italian family from Sicily. Chicago is my jurisdiction. He has no say here." Benito's dark, beady eyes looked like a rat's.

"Your affiliation put Lil's life at risk, and I won't have it." Max's voice never rose, but the threat was loud and clear. "You've also brokered a deal with the cartel, one that you are unable to fulfill—that makes your mistake a family issue."

"We'll vote," I proposed, wanting to put an end to the delusions Benito harbored and cut off the threat that would hurt only his family.

"All in favor of ending any and all business with the Espinosa cartel?" I counted out loud the raised hands. It was four to five, Rossi having joined in, something none of us doubted, as he openly opposed anything Benito did. "Majority rules. Should you go against the decision, there will be consequences to your inclusion as one of the five ruling families. You would risk the severing of the Chicago Brambilla family."

"That's extreme and not how we do things," Benito spat, disgust clear in his heated glare.

"Times are changing," Marco replied. "The decision holds."

We ignored Benito's sputtering as we stood from the table. I wanted to get back to Sofia. Her family needed her close while she healed, but I did as well. Soon, I would change things and remove the obstacles separating us.

After another few minutes to wrap up the meeting and arrange when the soldiers would swear fealty to Marco and me as the new bosses, we stood to leave. Benito led the pack, anger echoing in his heavy steps.

The metal door to the warehouse's parking lot was open. Benito exited the building as a shot rang out. He jerked, taking the bullet in his chest. He shifted to the side, falling to a knee behind one of the vehicles, and returned fire. We surged forward, guns out. Guards were stationed near the door we exited and helped to provide cover. Crouching by our parked cars, we waged our counterattack. There were five black sedans where the enemy drew a line of attack. My estimate put us at odds, only a handful short against their numbers. The question was whether we were facing off against cartel or Russians.

The heat of a bullet grazed my neck. My eyes narrowed as I targeted the source and aimed for his knee. When he dropped, I drilled a hole into his forehead then shifted to the man shielded by the driver's-side door. Same tactic, leg then headshot. A smile tugged at the corner of my lips, and I was reminded of how Sofia had used that method to eliminate the threat against her in Italy.

With that thought, a sense of urgency fueled me to my feet. *What if this is a setup, disguising a real attack against the girls?*

The same thought must have occurred to all of us except Frank and Benito, who didn't care about the women. They remained shielded by the cars as they fired back, keeping the risk to themselves to a minimum. Benito's arm rested on the hood of the car as he took shots. His color wasn't good, and blood dripped at a steady pace from his chest to splash against the ground near his feet.

The rest of us gained our feet, rapidly firing and ticking off the men who fell beneath our bullets. Two remained, and we made short work of them. Marco jogged over with Max close on his heels when the threat appeared to have been eliminated. Benito collapsed to the ground, and I wandered over to where Dino, his second, applied pressure to the chest wound. Blood pooled around his fingers, and Benito's white button-down was saturated with red. He was rapidly losing blood, and a gray cast painted his features with a grim prognosis for survival. The bullet looked to have pierced his heart.

Max stood over him, his gaze dispassionate and locked in on Benito. "That's unfortunate."

"Did someone call Trey?" Dino asked.

"No, and no one will," Max answered, sneering at Benito as he struggled for breath. "This wasn't how it was supposed to be. You were supposed to suffer. This is too quick."

Gurgles slipped past Benito's lips as we fanned around him. Dino lifted his gaze as the last few gasps escaped his boss's mouth. With a grim set to his features, Dino pronounced what we all had witnessed. "He's gone."

Max gave Dino a hand getting up. Once he was on his feet, he said what we were all thinking. "You'll oversee the Brambilla family, for now. We'll meet tomorrow and go over what the next steps are."

Dino nodded. I wondered how trustworthy he was, as Benito was as bad as Frank Rossi. I, for one, wasn't sad to see him go. Only one other boss stood in our way of ruling the Five Families into the future. Marco and Max got Benito's body into the back seat of the car Dino would drive. Funeral arrangements would be made in time.

"Who was behind the attack?" I asked Marco.

"Espinosa cartel." Marco frowned. "Raphe wasn't with them, but his son was. We'll need to get ahead of that."

I nodded. We would. But first, we had to check on the girls. "If Raphe wasn't with them, they could have divided. If this was a decoy, the real strike could be at our doorstep."

Nothing else needed to be said as we sprinted for the cars and peeled out of there. I barked a command into the car's Bluetooth to call Sofia. A sliver of calm infused my blood as she answered, her voice filled with laughter. They were okay for the time being. But there were other issues we would need to figure out. The biggest was how the cartel had known to strike where and when they had—who the rat in our family was.

CHAPTER TWENTY-SIX

ENZO

My skin itched with the need for action and the sense that what had happened at the warehouse was only a taste of the war to come. We would eliminate the cartel and teach them a lesson about who ruled Chicago to send back to their main branch in Colombia. They would not take us out or rule the city. We were shipping them back in body bags, and eventually, we would have to take the fight directly to the Colombians to eliminate the problem.

Max and Stefano would plan the attack we would unleash in an hour or less. No need to wait as they regrouped. Sofia, Em, and Lil were our priorities. My father and Marco would ensure nothing happened to the wives, and they'd argued for Sofia and the others to fall under their protection while we dealt with the recent threat. It was a good strategy, but I didn't think Sofia or Em would go for it. Lil might, but probably not if the others insisted on joining us.

I barreled through the La Rosas' front door, yelling for Sofia. I needed to see her, to know that she wasn't hurt. I raced through the foyer and down the hall in the direction of the theater room where they'd planned to be tonight. Max was on my heels.

There was no outward sign of invasion, no downed guards, no bullets in the drywall. I had no reason to think anything had happened to her, but I couldn't shake the fear. I needed to hold her in my arms to assure myself that she was safe and well.

My fingers closed around the door handle, and I yanked it open. A movie played on the screen, and four heads turned our way. I acknowledged my sister then ignored everyone except Sofia. They all got to their feet. Alarm widened Sofia's eyes. Em was next to her, and I grimaced as I addressed my sister. "Dad is in the foyer. You need to go home now."

Max had Lil in his arms. "Come on, Eva. We'll drop you at home."

She pursed lips but followed after Max and Lil without a word. I hugged Em then whispered in her ear, "Please hurry. Dad will take you home. The three of you should be spread out until we determine where the cartel will strike next."

"Cartel?" Em pulled back, confusion evident in the furrowing of her brows. "I thought the Russians were the concern."

"They are, but tonight, the Espinosa cartel attacked at the warehouse."

"Emiliana," our father called from the doorway, and I nudged her toward him.

Sofia threaded her fingers with mine, and I pulled her into my embrace, telling her everything that had happened. "We'll have a counterattack in"—I glanced at the time on my phone, noticing a text from her—"half an hour." I took a second to read it then gently moved her to arm's length. "What the hell is this about Katya?"

"Oh." A frown tugged at one side of her mouth, and she handed her phone to me, the texts between her and Katya open. "It wasn't what I wanted to find out, but maybe it will help to know what she thinks is coming. You told me Yuri gave lip service to peace between our families and theirs. But it doesn't appear that way from what Katya said."

I read the messages, appreciating the insight. Maybe Sofia was right, and Katya was an ally of sorts—a deadly one, though, and not to be blindly trusted. "We need to take care of the cartel first. Stefano can check in with his spies to see if the Russians are on the move."

"Stefano has spies watching the Russians? That's news to me."

I grinned. "Seems you have spies too."

The light laugh that spilled from Sofia's lips did us both a world of good. It was a bright spot in the uncertainty we would soon face.

"And Elena. It won't be long until she is with us again. And that means—"

"Nothing, Sof. Don't worry about something that hasn't happened. Let's focus on the cartel and the Russians. Those two issues are big enough."

I led her from the room, her hand in mine. I hated that I would have to leave her side, but the cartel needed to be taken care of. There was a lot I wanted to say to her, and I would when I was back. Robert rounded the corner, his wife's hand in his.

"I'm taking them to the safe room. Sofia, let's go."

"What?" She jerked her gaze to her dad. "Isn't that extreme?"

"Not when the Russians might attack, no," he answered.

Her lips formed an O, and she rose onto her toes, pressing a kiss to my cheek before following her parents. I watched her until she rounded the corner and left my sight. I couldn't take much more of us being separated—I wanted to live with her. Things would have to change very soon, and I already had a plan for how to do that.

I closed my eyes briefly. There hadn't been enough time. I

didn't even get to tell her Benito was dead, which I was sure Max felt cheated over. Then again, having Dino run things than report to Max would be better than Benito at the helm.

We were meeting at the house to go over a plan of attack. Marco appeared and waved me down a hallway until we stopped before a solid door with a keypad. Marco punched in some numbers, and the lock slid open with an audible pop. He swung the door wide, and we entered. Weapons were mounted on every available wall space. Trunks holding magazines and boxes of ammo lined the floor. Tactical gear was hung neatly on a rack and stacked on a section of shelving.

After we weaponed up, Stefano called. He and Max would meet us several blocks from the cartel's headquarters on the South Side of Chicago. We had half an hour to get there. I worried it was a trap, and the closer we got, the louder the voice in my mind became.

"Go back." Marco was driving. When he didn't immediately do as I said, I yelled at him to turn the fuck around.

"What's the problem?" he growled but complied.

I dialed Max and Stefano so I could explain to all of them at once. "This is the perfect setup for the Russians. While we're busy going after the cartel, they can attack our homes. It's too convenient. We can send enough soldiers to handle the cartel. We don't need to do it. That's Benito's mess and possibly orchestrated tonight by the Russians."

"Shit. That makes sense and is something I would do." Stefano cursed. "Max and I will arrange men to take over and attack the cartel. We'll get to Em and Lil in case they're targeted."

My gut said it wouldn't be them. "Grab Nicole." Elena was the adopted daughter of Nicole Caruso, and while Antonio was dead and Tony, his son, worthless, it made sense they would take her, since their objective had been about Elena. Rather than killing Nicole, abducting her might flush Elena out. But in terms of an eye for an eye, Sofia and I fell at the top of that list.

Marco floored it, and we flew down the highway back toward his house. I called my dad, while Marco used Bluetooth to do the same. The message was relayed, and I texted Sofia to make sure she was okay. We were lucky our fathers had stayed back with Marco's brothers. Sofia answered my text immediately.

Sofia: *That makes sense. Don't worry about me. In the panic room with Mom.*

Me: *We're five minutes out. What do you see on the monitors?*

Sofia: *Nothing. Wait—*

Sofia: *The house is dark. They're here.*

I relayed her message to Marco. We were minutes out, but a hell of a lot could happen during that time. The seconds dragged as we sped along the highway, weaving through the cars, taking the shoulder when necessary. Sweat trickled down my spine. I tapped the barrel of my gun against my thigh, waiting for the moment Marco pulled up to the house. The off-ramp came into view, and he took it at a speed that should have flung us off the road, but the car, thankfully, hugged the curve, leaving tire tracks in our wake. He ignored the traffic lights, and by some miracle, we made it to their street. Ten seconds out, I had two fingers on the door handle and the rest around my 9mm. We could hear the pop of gunfire, and as we skidded to a stop after running over two armed men wearing masks, I threw open the door and was out and firing.

All around the house, men fought or shot at each other. I recognized our men and focused on the others. From inside the house, in the upper windows, and on the roof, snipers eliminated the soldiers converging on ours. I spotted Robert on the second floor, picking off targets below with a high-powered rifle. Marco went left, firing his guns in fast succession.

The front door was open. Several men fought. Bodies

littered the steps. It was a fucking nightmare. Sidestepping a fight, I wove through the fallen men and let myself in. Inside the foyer, a dark form moved, knocking into my arm and almost making me drop my gun. The punch to my jaw knocked me back into another guy. I didn't recognize them. But one thing was clear: they weren't cartel. The retaliation I worried about was in effect. The men were Russians.

I angled my 9mm to point behind me then squeezed the trigger. The man holding me dropped, the bullet finding its mark. Free, I raised the gun to shoot the man in front of me. He kicked out a leg before I fired. Another of my weapons clattered across the floor. A grin stretched across his square jaw, and in his hand, he wielded a knife.

Moonlight aided our sight as we danced around one another, dodging and weaving. When the interior light momentarily blinded us, I jerked to the side, anticipating his move. He attacked, and I evaded. The flash of the blade came too close more than once. Twisting out of his way, I unsheathed a small knife I had.

I jolted to the side as the sharp prick from his weapon penetrated my side then lunged for his stomach. He clamped onto my wrist. I blocked his next strike with my free arm, twisted my hand, and shoved the blade through the underside of his exposed wrist while he still held mine.

The wound bought me a few seconds of him staring in disbelief at his skewered appendage. Locking my hand on his knife-wielding one, I relieved him of it and immediately plunged it into his chest. As he sputtered, slowly dropping to his knees, I lunged around him, picking up one of my guns as I went.

I had to get to Sofia. If they'd broken into the panic room where she was… I couldn't even finish that thought. The farther I traveled through the house, the less I heard the all-out war on the grounds. Then I saw four men working on the door to get inside the fortified room. I fired off a few shots, dropping two of them before the others turned, weapons in hand. I felt the impact of a bullet to my chest and another to my shoulder before I squeezed the rest of the ammo into their chests then heads.

My breathing hitched as the pressure in my chest spread. I released the empty magazine, retrieved a new one from my pocket, then slammed it home. I turned and plastered my back to the door, standing guard. The minutes ticked by slowly, and my eyelids grew heavy. I lost time as black spots invaded the edges of my sight, giving me tunnel vision.

I couldn't fail her. I had to stay conscious. A steady drip splashed on the ground, and it took me a few minutes to realize it was my blood. My legs gave out, and I sank to the floor. That was easier. I could rest my gun on my knee and still shoot anyone who came down the hall. Pain filtered through my body, but I blocked it.

A click sounded. I blinked, clearing the fog. Then I fell backward as the door opened. I lay at Sofia's feet. She cried out, and the last thing I experienced before I lost the battle to stay awake was my gun clattering to the floor and the sluggish panic that tried one last time to get my numb fingers to grasp it.

CHAPTER TWENTY-SEVEN

SOFIA

The door released after Mom put the correct code in, freeing us from the fortified room Dad made us go in while we were under attack. It was mostly over, and I had to get to Enzo. We saw the fight on the monitors. My heart nearly stopped beating when he was shot twice. Then he stood guard, bleeding all over the goddamned place.

When I pulled the door open, he could no longer stand. "Enzo!" I screamed when he fell flat onto the floor. I dropped to my knees beside him, applying pressure to the wounds on his chest. Mom stood over me, her gun covering us both while she talked to Trey, her phone pressed to her ear, describing what had happened.

I could barely breathe. My body trembled uncontrollably. *I can't lose him. I just got him back.* My world tunneled. There was only him. Everything slowed, and I stopped processing sound as I focused on the love of my life, who hung precariously in the balance.

His face was deathly pale, and his lips had a blueish cast to them. Blood covered my hands. Beneath them, his chest rose and fell, but I couldn't tell if his breathing was slowing. It was freaking me the hell out.

What am I going to do if he doesn't make it? "Come on, Enzo. Open your eyes." No response. I wasn't above begging. "Please don't leave me." Tears leaked from my eyes and splashed onto him. "I love you." Someone pulled me back, and I let out a guttural cry. "What are you doing?"

Blinking rapidly, Trey came into focus as he bent over Enzo. Sound returned with a punishing snap: the random pop of a gun firing, someone screaming in the distance, then Marco's voice.

"Sof, stop it." Marco held me tightly, my back to his chest, his arms a steel band that kept me from clawing my way back to Enzo. "Trey is working on him. You need to give him space."

I ceased struggling. Trey barked orders to lift Enzo to a nearby table. Marco and I followed. Mom wasn't far behind. When we stopped, she clasped my hand. Marco never let go of me, keeping an arm around my shoulders, either for support or to keep me from running to Enzo—I couldn't say which.

In silence, with tremors wracking my body and tears streaming down my face, we watched while Trey cleaned the wounds. He ordered a couple of our men to get what he needed while he set up an IV. Next, he removed the bullets, stitched the skin, and applied bandages.

When Trey turned to me, his face grim, I fell apart again. I wasn't sure I wanted to hear what he would say. His face said it was bad. It looked bad. There was so much blood. My knees buckled, and Marco's grip tightened so I didn't fall.

I lost time, unable to tell how much or little had passed. After a while, I gained my legs back, locking my knees. Marco released me, asking if I would be okay. I nodded but didn't let go of Mom's hand. She stayed with me even as Enzo was moved to a guest bedroom on the main floor. She smoothed my hair, kissing the top of my head and murmuring that he would be fine. When she hugged me and said she needed to find Dad, I let her go, transferring my death grip to Enzo's hand.

Dropping my forehead to our clasped hands, I clung to him. "You can't leave me. I have plans for us. The house in Mondello? That was supposed to be for us. I wasn't going to buy a separate one. *You claimed me.* You told me you love me. You can't take it back. I won't let you." I sucked in a breath, my rant far from over. His blood covered my hands, and I placed my scarred palm flush against the one on his from our oath when we were kids. "And Elena can't have you. I don't give a damn about some stupid contract. She left. I'm here. And you're mine. Please, Enz, come back to me."

Eventually, I climbed into bed, careful not to jostle him. My head rested against his good shoulder, and I wrapped my hand around his. Trey came back and checked his vitals and changed out his IV bag.

"You know he'll be fine, Sof, right? He'll wake up soon."

A few more tears slipped from the corners of my eyes, and my lips trembled. "Thank you."

Trey rounded to my side of the bed and pressed a kiss on my head before leaving. The fight must have ended a long time ago, and I was vaguely aware that I hadn't asked if there were any other injuries—or worse, fatalities. But I couldn't bring myself to muster up the energy to go find out. My eyelids shut, and a wave of exhaustion hit me hard.

I must have dozed. When I slowly blinked my eyes, panic shocked me fully awake with the reality of why I was lying in bed next to Enzo. I sucked in a breath, terrified that he'd stopped breathing. Over several seconds, I took stock of my surroundings and how his hand was warm in mine. Then the steady rise and fall of his chest eased my fear.

"I was wondering when you would wake up." His voice was rough.

"Enzo." I took care to sit up without causing the bed to move too much. "How are you feeling?"

"Fine." That familiar grin curved his lips, the sexy one that showed a hint of a dimple on his cheek. "So you were worried about me?"

"What the hell were you doing? I was fine. They weren't getting through the door." I crossed my arms over my chest. With him awake and the crisis averted, I let my fear-fueled temper loose. "You risked your life unnecessarily and scared me."

He chuckled then tugged at my waist. "Come here."

I went. There was no way I wouldn't have. He made room for me to snuggle against him, my head resting on his shoulder, while he held me close. I tangled my legs with his and wrapped my arm around his waist. The trembling returned, and with it, all the emotions I'd been battling since he was shot. "I love you so goddamned much, Enzo. Please don't leave me again."

"I'm not going anywhere. I love you, too, Sofia."

We lay together, dozing on and off. Nothing mattered but being in each other's arms.

Enzo

I hated to leave Sofia while she slept, but I needed to take care of something. It was an obstacle between us that I could tell caused her immense stress, and I couldn't have that. The gunshot wasn't a big deal. I'd lost a lot of blood. That was the problem. Sure, it sucked, and I was sore as hell, but it wasn't fatal. I woke her enough to let her know that I would be back. She protested and snuggled closer, making it hard to want to leave the bed. But I had to. And when she fell back into a deep sleep, I did.

Marco met me not far from the room I had been in with a grunt. "Good to see your lazy ass is out of bed."

I laughed, and my chest protested with a sharp twinge of pain. "I woke Sofia and told her I would be back, but I'm not sure if she'll remember when she gets up. Make sure she does."

"Like I answer to you." Marco shook his head, but amusement danced through his eyes before they sobered with a darker emotion. "Do not hurt my sister."

"That's the last thing I want to do. There's just something that I need to take care of so I can make sure that won't happen."

"Then get on with it." Marco slapped me on the shoulder farthest from my injury.

It still fucking hurt. I sucked in a painful breath. *Asshole*. I took pleasure in the fact that he didn't know how much his world would change, and very soon. The secret Sofia and I held would alter everything, and I was going to sit back and watch with popcorn.

"Have you or Robert talked with Yuri?" I needed it done so there wouldn't be further attacks.

He nodded. "We told him that Benito died, crippling one of the arms of the Five Families." A wicked smile curved his lips, and I laughed.

A cartel kill had caused his death, but switching it up and using it as retribution to appease the Russian boss was a genius move. "Did it work?"

"Like gold—an eye for an eye. Yuri seemed pleased, and with what Ivan did to Sofia, he'd agreed to return to peace between the families."

"Since when did we have peace between the Russians and us?"

"Let's just say that we're back to what we were."

"Good enough for me." I turned to leave with a lighter step. That was one major problem averted. Benito's death had given us the scapegoat we'd needed. And while the Brambilla family was hurting, it wasn't crippled, as Marco had grossly embellished.

With Marco, Max, and I in charge of our families, we would need to figure out who would ultimately control the Brambilla arm, aside from the temporary Band-Aid we'd put in place with Dino running it and reporting to Max. We were almost Five Families strong. The only other problem was the Rossi family. We needed Stefano to take over for our plan for a unified front to come to fruition. But that was a worry for another day.

As I made my way through the house, there weren't bodies littering the floor or grounds any longer. Sunlight met me when I stepped outside. I hadn't been aware of how long Sofia and I'd slept.

I passed soldiers carrying a random body or two, staff cleaning, and Robert, who stopped to make sure I was well and inform me that my family had been kept abreast of my situation. I had to roll my eyes at that. It was a scratch. The blood loss and unconsciousness were embarrassing. Robert knew that, and his laughter followed me as I got into my car and pulled away.

The drive helped to clear my head. And after about twenty minutes, I was at Max and Lil's lakefront condo, where they had gone the night before. The home they were building wasn't yet complete.

He was expecting me, and the gate swung open so I could park in the secured underground parking area. The rhythmic sound of the waves followed me to the elevator. I rode it to their floor. When the doors opened, Max was waiting in the living room.

I glanced around. "Where's Lil?"

"Sleeping." Max indicated for me to follow him down a hallway and into his office, where he motioned for me to close the door. The room was well lit with the floor-to-ceiling blinds open. We had a stellar view of the lake. Bookshelves lined one wall, a credenza and shelves bisecting them. A decanter of amber alcohol with four tumblers was among the sparsely decorated counter. "How's the..." He waved toward my chest.

"It's nothing." He settled behind his mahogany desk, and I sat across from him, annoyed by how tense I was. But it meant everything to me, to us. I only hoped Max would be sympathetic. "You hold all of Antonio's documents, his contracts."

Understanding lit in Max's gaze, but he only nodded. "That's not a problem anymore."

Sofia would kill me, at least initially, for telling Max and breaking her trust, at least until she heard why I'd done it. It was hard to believe that Max, whom I'd only met fleetingly in Italy and hadn't remembered when he covertly came to Chicago, was the Caruso boss. I only hoped that worked in my favor. It had to.

"You're happy with Lil." I was stalling, but I wanted him to be one hundred percent on the same page and feeling everything he did for Lil when I put him in my shoes.

Max's gaze turned wary. "You know I am. She's everything to me. Where is this going?"

I grunted. "That feeling is where I'm going. The one where you want to wake every morning to her smile and to go to sleep at night with her in your arms... that's the one I'm talking about." I wasn't planning to detail each aspect of how the women in our lives were our other halves or that neither of us would want to go on if they weren't in it. Because I knew the devastation, the sheer magnitude of the monster living inside of me that would be unleashed on the world if anything took her from me. It was something I knew Max shared by the way I'd witnessed him behave around Lil.

"What I don't understand is why you're talking about that. What does how I feel for my wife has anything to do with you?"

"As the Caruso boss, you've inherited all the contracts,

including an arranged marriage one between me and one of your sisters."

Max's brows furrowed. "I'm a little lost here. That contract is null and void, because my adopted sister isn't alive any longer. There is nothing stopping you from marrying Sofia. I'm assuming that's what this is about."

"Yes, but there is something stopping me." *Forgive me, Sof, for telling Max when you told me not to say anything. It's for a damn good reason.* "Elena is alive."

Max froze, his hand curling into a fist on the top of the desk. "What the hell do you mean, Elena is alive? She's been living a nightmare for the past four years?" He stood, looming over me, fury crackling in the air between us. "We gave up looking for her when we when we found the destroyed building, and in it, her DNA."

Fuck. Wrong way to break it to him. I went into detail about what Sofia had shared with me, including Katya's connection. "We plan to return her to the fold in a couple of weeks, which means—"

"That the contract is still in effect." Max resumed his seat, his gaze speculative.

I took a deep breath, prepared to offer my soul to be with Sofia. "I love Sofia. I can't marry Elena." My hands were damp, but I refused to rub them along the top of my slacks and telegraph the extent of my nervousness. "If you dissolve the contract, I will owe you a favor."

"Elena will need protection when she returns. Hold off on bringing her back unless she is in immediate danger. I'll have to find someone else to take your place and arrange her marriage."

"You'll dissolve my contract, then?" I stood, needing to loosen my tense muscles and because I wanted to get back to her. "I'm free to marry Sofia?"

Max rose as well then went to a black filing cabinet hidden behind a panel. After unlocking it, he withdrew a few papers.

When he faced me again, he showed me the arranged-marriage contract and then tore it up. "Lil would murder me if I stood in the way of her best friend's happiness. You can marry Sofia, but I will keep that favor for a later date."

I nodded. Thanking him, I got the hell out of there. I didn't even care what he wanted, so long as I had her. And for the first time since Sofia had told me Elena was alive and that the contract was intact, I could see my future, and it was fucking fabulous because I would have the love of my life by my side.

CHAPTER TWENTY-EIGHT

ENZO

Two weeks later…

"Where are you taking me?" Sofia asked for the third time.

I grinned then pulled her into my lap. "It's supposed to be a surprise, even though you'll figure out where soon enough."

She sighed then leaned against me, her loose braid hanging over one shoulder. I put on the romantic comedy she'd talked about over the past few days. It would distract her for a little while.

We'd boarded the jet after I met with the Vitale soldiers. Fealty was sworn, again by my father in front of our family, officially establishing me as the Vitale boss. He and Mom were happy. They, as well as Marco and Sofia's parents, had several trips planned. Retirement was a reward after the intensity of the life we lived. They would get pulled back into business from time to time, but it afforded them a certain amount of freedom they hadn't had before.

I'd gone to pick her up around one in the morning. Her mom was in on it and had a bag already packed. Sofia was asleep, and I'd carried her to the car, where she'd stirred awake momentarily until she realized it was me. Hours passed in the air, and it wasn't until she awoke the next morning that the questions about how I'd gotten her on the jet began. She'd been drinking with the girls—that was how.

"How do you feel now that you're boss?" She tilted her head back to meet my eyes.

"About the same, just with a hell of a lot more responsibility." But it was good. I'd met with Max, Stefano, and Marco the night before. Changes were coming soon after Sofia and I returned from our mini vacation that consisted of a mere four days. Then we would implement the next phase to make our families stronger, including bringing Elena back—a discussion Sofia and I needed to have. Katya hadn't contacted her, but I thought she might. There was more to Elena's story that we didn't know, and it seemed that Katya did.

Another thing we'd settled on was that we needed a *capo dei capi*, a boss of all bosses, something the Sicilians did not recognize. But for the Five Families in the Chicago Mafia, it was necessary for what we wanted to establish with our new ruling members. Max and I already had someone in mind for that position, but that man didn't know it yet. There would be lots of changes, big ones, and I was looking forward to the ride.

We began the descent, and Sofia got off my lap to return to her seat. "So… Mondello?"

I laughed. "Yeah. It's been pretty stressful for both of us with the Ivan nightmare then the attack a few weeks ago, and we have yet to uncover the rat in the family. We could use a break."

"How long do we have until you're needed back home?"

"Four days."

"I can't wait." She smiled, and her eyes sparkled with excitement.

The jet touched down, and soon, we were taxiing on the runway then off the plane and into a car. We passed the time talking about the house in our neighborhood in the States that I'd purchased and what ideas she had for the interior. She'd toured it two days before and had already sketched a few plans. She thought it was my place. It wasn't. It was ours, and she would know that soon enough.

We pulled up to the house in Modello. I got out of the car as she said, "I don't understand."

I opened her door then took her hand and helped her out. "It's ours, Sof."

She whirled around and splayed her palms flat on my chest. "You found a place?"

"For us."

Confusion marred her face. "How is that possible?"

"Max released me from the marriage contract."

Her eyes went wide. "Enzo."

I took advantage of her speechless state, grasped one of her hands, and led her to the door. It was a white one-story villa with black storm shutters and a one-hundred-eighty-degree view of the sea. There was a deck and pool in the back.

It was in the mid-seventies that late October day, which was perfect. I didn't think either of us would ever care what the weather was if we were there. The area was breathtaking. When my gaze dropped to hers, I realized it wasn't the landscape that was so stunning but the woman in my embrace. She eclipsed everything.

She looped her arms around my neck and tugged so that I bent and captured her lips with mine. The kiss was everything that was us: familiarity, intensity, love, and passion. I could easily have lost myself in her if not for the house she undoubtedly wanted to see. She broke the kiss, and I let her for the time being.

When she slid her hands down my chest, I grabbed them and

tugged her toward the front door, not that she required any encouragement to go inside. But I needed the distraction of viewing the house before I let my desire for her run away.

After unlocking the door, I pushed it wide. With my hand resting on the small of her back, we went in to see the open-concept dining room, living room, and kitchen. Light spilled through the windows and bounced off the marble-tiled floor. Sofia gasped at the panoramic view of the Adriatic Sea from the accordion glass doors at the back of the house that overlooked the pool and would enable indoor-outdoor living by folding them back.

"I didn't have it furnished because I thought you would want to do that." My voice echoed through the unfurnished space. "There's a room that's perfect for a design studio, and since we'll be in Italy at least once I year, I thought you would need it. One thing we'll update is the back area. The pool is outdated, and there's no hot tub."

She squealed and threw her arms around me. "I love that you thought about me with the studio. I have plans already. And this view... I can't believe you found the place. How?" She whirled around.

I could practically see the ideas swirling in her mind. "The couple who owned it were in their eighties and didn't have any children. The upkeep was too much, and they wanted to move closer to the town where most of their friends live. We offered them a hundred thousand over asking, all cash, and they jumped at it. Now, it's ours."

She worried her lower lip with her teeth, and I guided her to the back deck, where I wanted her. We stood for a moment, taking in the view. Whitecaps danced over the sea from a small storm that would arrive in a little less than an hour. Above us, there wasn't a cloud in the sky, but darkness gathered along the horizon. It was reminiscent of our lives—we had pockets of peace and beauty before all hell broke loose. And I wouldn't have wanted it any other way because I appreciated the beauty all the more.

With my finger under her chin, I urged her to look at me. "You're so beautiful, Sof." The years played through my mind on a fast reel. "I think I fell in love with you when I was eight. You were sweet and would go along with whatever game your brothers and I would play without complaint."

She chuckled. "Unless my clothes were messed up."

My grin stretched impossibly wide. "True. You were insane about your clothes. It was an instant trigger from perfect to crazy in one point two seconds flat. No one wanted to be around then. I think all of us would prefer to take on a dozen armed men than your wrath."

She shrugged. "It's a skill."

"I love every part of you, even that frightening side." I winked then took both her hands in mine. "I've been lucky enough to have you as my best friend growing up, even if I didn't always recognize how close we were or how integral you are to my happiness. I'm aware of that now, and I'll never take you for granted."

Tears misted over her pretty amber eyes, and the slight tremble in her lower lip tugged at my heart. Our lives were bound together and had been since we took that blood oath when she was six and I was eight.

"Everything I do, from buying this house to following you to Fashion Week in Milan each year, is for you, and I wouldn't have it any other way. Even though you already are in my heart, I have to ask, if only to shout it to the rest of the world so they'll know it too… will you be my wife?"

"Yes," she whispered then laughed with tears streaming down her flushed cheeks. She pushed her scarred palm against my identical mark, sealing us together like we'd done when we were young. "I wouldn't have it any other way, Enz. My heart has always been yours, and when I imagine my future, you're always by my side."

I slipped the eight-carat emerald-cut diamond ring on her finger.

She sucked in a breath and held as the stone caught the light. "It's beautiful."

"No more so than you." My mouth descended on hers, and she met my kiss eagerly and with the same intensity. In the distance, thunder rumbled, and I gentled the caress, tilting her head then slanting my mouth over hers, deepening the kiss. My hands went to her waist, lifting her. She complied by hopping up and wrapping her legs around me. I broke the kiss long enough to carry her inside and to the bedroom, where I'd had the sense to have a king-sized bed delivered. That much I was confident in ordering myself. The rest of the house she would decorate and make a home for us, an oasis for the times we could get away from Chicago and focus only on us.

As the storm drew closer and the sky darkened with a flash of lightning in the distance, we fell onto the bed. We enjoyed one another because we knew when to make the most of our time, especially with a storm on the horizon, literally and figuratively. But with Sofia by my side, I could handle whatever came our way.

Continue reading the Mafia Elite series with Born in Darkness: https://amymckinleyauthor.com/mafia-elite/

If you enjoyed reading BLOOD OATH as much as I did writing it, I hope you'll consider leaving a review.

Her enemies are his, and when Emiliana's life is threatened, Stefano takes matters into his own hands to ensure her safety. As they grow closer, so do their enemies. But he's ready for them. Nothing will keep him from Emiliana, and he'll slay anyone who threatens what's his.

215

Continue reading the Mafia Elite series with Born in Darkness: https://amymckinleyauthor.com/mafia-elite/

ACKNOWLEDGMENTS

This series has been so fun to write! And of course, I have a fantastic group of people to thank for being there, from start to finish, of Blood Oath's creation. I am fortunate to have these incredible women and authors share their input, support, and encouragement. Emily Albright, Kristin Kisska, and Candace Irvin. My editors, Kate Birdsall and Taylor Anhalt, helped shape this story into what it is today. Then there is my family, my husband, and four kids. I am so grateful for their support.

Thank you to T.E. Black Designs, who always exceeds my expectations. Colleen Noyes with Itsy Bitsy Book Bits, and Danielle Sanchez with Wildfire Marketing Solutions, are outstanding. I'm lucky to have them in my corner, working their magic to make each release a success.

Last but certainly not least, a special thank you to all the bloggers and readers who have encouraged and helped me along the way and who continue to make my dream a reality.

Thank you.

ABOUT THE AUTHOR

Amy McKinley is the *USA Today* best-selling author of the romantic suspense thriller Gray Ghost Novels, Deadly Isles Special Ops, Covert Recruits, Mafia Elite, Moonlit Destination Series, the Five Fates paranormal romance books, and several standalone titles. Her edge-of-your-seat books are filled with surprising twists and just the right amount of heat and danger. She lives in Illinois with her husband, two daughters, two sons, and three mischievous cats.

You can find her at:
www.AmyMcKinley.com

Subscribe to Amy's newsletter for cover reveals, book announcements, and giveaways:
http://eepurl.com/dEBqJn

facebook.com/amymckinleyauthor
bookbub.com/authors/amy-mckinley
instagram.com/amymckinleyauthor
twitter.com/AmyMcKinley7

Katya

Standalone Titles

Shattered Melody

Siren's Call: Cursed Seas

Fake Fiancé (A Second Chance Office Romance)

Moonlit Destination Series

Moonlit Whisper

Moonlit Kiss

Moonlit Mirage

Five Fates Series

Hidden

Taken

www.ingramcontent.com/pod-product-compliance
Lightning Source LLC
Chambersburg PA
CBHW070939190726
48292CB00004B/1249